I0608780

Charles Perrin Smith

Lineage of the Lloyd and Carpenter Family

compiled from authentic sources

Charles Perrin Smith

Lineage of the Lloyd and Carpenter Family
compiled from authentic sources

ISBN/EAN: 9783337369354

Printed in Europe, USA, Canada, Australia, Japan

Cover: Foto ©Andreas Hilbeck / pixelio.de

More available books at **www.hansebooks.com**

Lineage

OF THE

Lloyd and Carpenter

FAMILY.

Compiled from Authentic Sources

By Charles Perrin Smith,

Trenton, N. J.

For Circulation among the Branches of the Family Interested.

Printed by S. Chew, Camden.
1870.

*E ?
L 172

Entered according to Act of Congress, in the year 1870, by

CHARLES P. SMITH,

In the Clerk's Office of the District Court of the United States, for the District of New Jersey.

TO the descendants of THOMAS LLOYD and SAMUEL CARPENTER I need offer no apology for this volume, as I rely upon the expressed wishes of relatives and friends, and the interest which all are supposed to take in their ancestry. In transcribing the remarkable genealogy, and throughout the work, I was necessarily restricted to such reliable authorities as were of convenient access, and it is a subject of regret that my almost incessant public duties precluded farther research. It is proper to add that the work was compiled for my immediate family, without expectation of its appearing in print, and a limited edition only has been issued for private circulation among those interested in the descent.

I desire most fully to express my obligations to JOHN JAY SMITH, Esq., of Germantown, (a descendant of Governor Thomas Lloyd,) for placing at my disposal his "*History of the Hill Family,*" embracing not only the genealogy, but a large amount of interesting information in reference to the Lloyd branch; to LLOYD P. SMITH, Esq., of the Philadelphia Library, for Burke's volumes, "*The Landed Gentry of Great Britain,*" in which the genealogy of the Lloyd family is published; to SAMUEL PRESTON CARPENTER, Esq., of Salem; Hon. JOHN CLEMENT, of Haddonfield; WILLIAM H. SNOWDEN, Esq., of Mount Vernon Estate, Virginia; HARPER & BROTHERS, of New York; J. B. LIPPINCOTT, Esq., of Philadelphia, and others, for facilities cheerfully afforded.

CHARLES PERRIN SMITH.

TRENTON, N. J., June, 1870.

THE CARPENTER MANSION, OR "SLATE-ROOF HOUSE."

AS IT APPEARED IN 1700.

Introductory.

THE ancient people of Britain were called in their own language, "Cymri." The name of Britons was conferred by the Romans from "Prydain" or "Britain." They are usually termed Welshmen, from the old Saxon "Wilise," an adjective signifying anything foreign: hence Italy is the Welshland of modern Germans—foreigners—as the Britons were to the old English or Anglo Saxon invaders. The Britons were brave and sturdy warriors, and if they had made common cause, the Romans might not have prevailed against them. JULIUS CÆSAR was the first civilized stranger who invaded the Island, B. C., 52: but his incursions were confined to the southern coast, and the Roman dominion did not attain its full extent in Britain until CNÆUS JULIUS AGRICOLA, took command, A. D., 78. The Romans did not conquer the more remote parts beyond the Friths of Forth and Clyde. The Britons soon adopted and emulated the customs of the Roman conquerors: they learned to speak the Latin language, adopted Latin names, clad themselves in rich raiment, and vied with the Romans in every luxury of corrupted Rome. The real power of the Roman government was in the sword. When the Empire began to decline, the Romans, as well as the Britons, were incessantly exposed to the hostility of the Picts. These were originally Britons, who lived beyond the Roman frontier, and had long continued in the enjoyment of their independence. The first inroad of the Picts, (A. D., 306,) was repelled: but when the Scots arrived from the opposite coast of Erin, the union of the forces enabled them to pursue their operations with great success. They rushed from the North like a torrent, attacked and plundered London; and though the invasion was repelled by Theodosius, A. D., 367 and 368, still the northern districts were never afterwards reduced. The Scots were the relatives of the Cymri, who at an early period established themselves in Hibernia, Erin, or Ireland; hence that Island, from its predominant population was generally called Scotia. The name of Scotia, or Scotland, as applied to the northern portion of Britain, is of comparatively modern origin. Flocking from settlements upon the coast, or passing from beyond the seas, the Saxons joined the Picts and Scots in their great invasion.

While these events were taking place in Britain, hordes of barbarians were pouring into Gaul and Italy. The Romans were compelled to abandon Britain, (A. D., 406 and 418,) and at length the connection was suddenly severed. Britain broke into various independent and rival communities, and the petty sovereigns contended among themselves for empire. Then followed the Saxon invasion, and conquest by "the three tribes of Germany," called the Jutes, the Angles and the Saxons. Ship after ship arrived, filled with eager warriors. The Britons were defeated with great slaughter. After various battles, and conquests of different sections of the country, *the noblest of the Britons maintained themselves in Cambria,* or Wales. Thus reads the history:

"The Anglo Saxons more than once overran their country; but the Cymri defended themselves amidst their fastnesses. They detested the Saxons, *and would not conform to the Saxon customs or laws.* The Romanized Britons appear to have more readily united with their invaders. *In the Kingdoms or Principalities of the Western Cymri, the old lines or dynasties of the Princes continued unbroken;* MANY SUBSIST IN THE NOBILITY AND GENTRY OF WALES AT THE PRESENT DAY; *and the whole body of the people continue in the possession of their native soil, unmingled with the stranger.*"

[The foregoing historical compilation, from standard authorities, but more especially from "*Palgrave's History of the Anglo Saxons,*" (London, 1831,") is an appropriate preface to the remarkable Genealogical Record about to be transcribed. As it refers to the reign of KING ARTHUR, A. D. 517, it is equally appropriate to insert the following brief sketch of that monarch and his times:]

THE life and deeds of KING ARTHUR have been so involved in fiction that it is not an easy task to give a definite account of him. He reigned in the beginning of the Sixth Century. NENNIUS says that he gained twelve victories over the Saxons. CEDRIC, the Saxon, was his great opponent. MORDRED, his nephew, revolted from him, which brought on the fatal battle of Comlan in Cornwall, in 542, where MORDRED was slain, and ARTHUR mortally wounded. The British Celts long believed that he would one day come back, and lead them again to drive the Sassenach into the sea, and vindicate for the Celtic race the undivided sovereignty of Britain. Other accounts state that he drove the Scots and Picts back to their Highland fastnesses, destroyed the Pagan temples of the Saxons, and restored Christianity. The following year he conquered Iceland, and annexed it. Then ensued twelve years of peace. Ten years more were occupied in making conquests in Gaul and Norway. Returning to Britain he held a great gathering at Caerlon, in Monmouthshire, where tributary Kings attended him. The Romans demanding tribute, he passed through Gaul, and was preparing to cross the Alps

to attack them, when the revolt of his nephew MORDRED (who had formed an alliance with the Saxons, Scots and Picts,) recalled him. He established an Order renowned in song and story, as the "*Knights of the Round Table*," and surrounded his Court with the utmost of barbaric splendor.

Tennison, Spencer, and others, have delved deeply into the lore of this romantic age, and passed in review the beautiful but erring Queen Gunievere, Launcelot the Knight peerless, the lists of Camelot, and all the knightly deeds of the Table Round.

"THE Kymry, a Celtic tribe, who emigrated from the Continent before the historic period, were in possession of nearly the whole of South Britain when the Romans first visited the country, having driven their ancient enemies, the Gaels, into Scotland, Ireland, the Hebrides, and the Isle of Man. They were continually harassed, *but never wholly conquered by the Romans*, who succeeded in driving them into the countries west of the Severn (Wales,) and established some camps in their territory. The Anglo Saxons subsequently found them formidable enemies, *but could never dislodge them from their mountain fastnesses*."—*New American Cyclopædia*, Vol. XVII, p 174.

"THE Welch are descendants from the ancient Britons, who in the conquest of England by the Saxons, sought refuge among the mountains of Cambria, or Wales. Many of the inhabitants speak the ancient language. They are much attached to their native hills, and are proud of their early origin."—*From Mitchell's Great Britain.*

JOHN BURKE, Esq., the Genealogist, from whose "*History of the Landed Gentry of Great Britain*," the following Lineage of the LLOYD FAMILY is extracted:

"SIR JOHN BERNARD BURKE, an English Genealogist, born in London, 1814. His father the late JOHN BURKE, who died in 1848, was a cadet of an ancient family in Ireland, and became attached as editor and reporter to the London press. * * * * He was the founder and joint editor (latterly assisted by his two sons,) of "*Burke's Peerage and Baronetage*," long established as the most complete and accurate of its class, and so popular that a new edition is annually exhausted. In May 1857, the copyright was sold for a large sum, although burthened with the payment of £400, to whichever of Mr. Burke's sons should edit the "*Peerage*" as long as it continued to be published. Mr. BURKE also brought out "*The Extinct Peerage*," "*The General Armory of England, Scotland and Ireland*," and "*The History of the Landed Gentry*." Sir BERNARD BURKE, called to the English Bar at the Middle Temple in 1839, succeeded him as editor of the "*Peerage*," and has also brought out revised and extended editions of his other works."—*New American Cyclopædia.*

GENEALOGY

OF THE

Lloyd Family.

From "Burke's History of the Landed Gentry of Great Britain," by John Burke, *Esq.,*
4 vols : London, 1838.

Esto Vigilans.

ARMS :	ESTATES :
Quarterly 1st & 4th, Sa.	In the counties of
A he-Goat passant, arg:	WARWICK
2d and 3d, az; three	and
Cocks, arg; armed &c:	STAFFORD,
or.	Crest—a he-Goat.

An extended Coat of Arms to which the name of CHARLES LLOYD is attached, was taken from a panel in DOLOBRAN HALL, 1780, and having been engraved, a copy was sent to JOSEPH P. NORRIS, by FRANCIS LLOYD, Esq. of Birmingham, England, in 1826. It is as follows:—(*Hist. of Hill Family.*)

FIFTEEN QUARTERINGS:

1. ⅓ Gu. A Chev. ar. between three Cocks.
   ⅔ Sa. A Chev. ar. charged with a Talbot's head, and two stars between three lamps.
2. Sa. Three Griffin's heads erased.
3. Sa. and ar. Charged with a Lion rampant.
4. Ar. A Lion passant, sa. between three *fleur de lis*—two and one.
5. ⅓ Gu. A Lion ar. passant.
   ⅔ Ar. A Lion sa. passant.
6. Or. A Lion gu. rampant.
7. Er. A Lion sa. rampant.
8. Gu. A Chev. ar. between three Cocks.
9. Gu. Two Lions passant, one above the other.
10. Er. and sa. A Lion or. rampant.
11. Az. A bordure engrailed or. charged with three Griffin's heads, erased gu.
12. ⅓ Three Boars' heads.
    ⅔ Gu. A Lion, or. rampant.
13. Sa. A Chev. ar. between two Owls.
14. Ar. A Lion sa. Ducally crowned, rampant.
15. Az. A dagger, or. point downwards.

Crest. A Cock, combed, beaked and wattled.

Lloyd of Dolobran.

LINEAGE.

This ancient family was established in Montgomeryshire about the middle of the Sixth Century. From

1. **Meirig,** the first on record, descended his eldest son

2. **Sawl,** and then in succession

3. **Lynam.**

4. **Llewelyn.**

5. **Seisyllt.**

6. **Lowarch.**

7. **Collwyn,** Prince of Demeea, or Dimetia, a tract of country around Myvod, consisting of part of Merionethshire and Montgomeryshire. He bore az. three Cocks, arg. armed, crested, and jilloped, or.

8. **Gwyn,** Prince of Dyfed.

9. **Gwrgant.**

10. **Ivor.**

* Surnames were introduced by the Normans about the year 1000.

11. **Llewellyn.**

12. **Cadwgan.**

13. **Griffith.**

14. **Cadwgan.**

15. **Aleth,** Prince of Dyfed.

16. **Aleth,** Lord of Dyfed, who was living in the eleventh Century. He married Nest (Agnes,) daughter of Llewellyn, ap Gwrgant, Prince of Morganwg and Glamorgan.

17. **Wrborgd,** Prince of Dyfed, who married Genhwyfar, daughter of Cadivor, Lord of Blaeneych, Caermarthenshire, usually styled Cadivor *Vaur*. or Cadivor the Great.

18. **Iertweth,** Lord of Falgarth, married (A. D. 1112) ELLEN, daughter of UCHDRYD EDWYN, Prince of Fegengl.

19. **Georgenen,** married ALES, daughter of GRONWY ap. Enion ap. Llewarch, Cynhaelthwy, descended from URIEN, Lord of Reged, a district in South Wales.

20. **Gwerfgl,** married JESWERTH, daughter and heiress of John ap. Cynric Vychan *ap Cynric ap Llawarch ap Keilin*, descended from *Muerchweithian*. Chief of one of the fifteen tribes of Wales, and by her had a son, Owen Noel, of Pencelli, in South Wales, and of Arwysth, in North Wales. He married secondly, EVA, daughter of Sir ARON AP RYS AP BLEDRI, "Knight of the Sepulchre." *Sir Aron* was a Crusader with RICHARD *Cœur de Lion*. By Eva he was father of

21. **Cynddelw,** who married JANE, daughter of Gwrwared, Lord of Cemes in South Wales.

22. **Ririd ap Cynddelw,** married Gwladys (Claudia,) daughter and heiress of Rivid, Lord of Llwydiarth, in Powysland—one of the sons of Cyric Efel, Lord of Eylwyseyl, in North Wales.

23. **Celynyn** of Llwydiarth, (he bore for arms, " *sable*, a he-goat attired and langued *or*." Many of his descendants bear as a crest, a holly tree, ppr. on a mount vert, a he-goat arg. attired or, browsing on the tree, which he holds with his two fore feet. This crest is borne by some as arms on a shield sa.) ... A Celynyn of Llwydiarth married Gwenllian, daughter of Meredith ap Rhydderch, descended from Tewdwr Maur (or Theodore *the Great*,) Prince of South Wales.

24. **Enion ap Celynyn** Llwydiarth, married Gwenllian, daughter of Adda ap Meiric, of Mochorant, son of Cynric ap Pasgen ap Cywyn, Lord of Guilsfield, descended from Brochwel Prince of Powys.

25. **Llewellyn ap Enion,** of Llwydiarth, married *Llenci* (Lucy,) daughter of Griffith Lloyd, of Bromfield, in Flintshire, son of *Ednyfed Lloyd* of Maelor, descended from *Earls of Hereford*. LLEWELLYN divided his estates among his children, giving Llwydiarth and Llanihangel to his eldest son, and his lands in Myvod and Dolobran to his second son *David*, who married *Meddefys*, daughter of *Griffith Deuddur*, descended from *Brochwel*, Prince of Powys, and was father of

26. **Ivan Teg,** (or the handsome,) of Dolobran, who married *Mawd,* daughter of *Evan Blaney,* of Tregynon and Castle Blaney, in the county of Monaghan, Ireland, ancestor of the Lords Blaney.

> IVAN TEG assumed the name of *Lloyd,* about the year 1476, from Lloydiarth, the seat of his grandfather. He had two sons—DAVID (his heir.) and *Owen.* Owen married *Katharine,* daughter of *Meredith Kinault* ap *Sir Griffith Vaughn,* and was father of *Evan Lloyd,* who married Gwenhwfar, daughter of *Meredith Lloyd,* of Nevoid, and had a son, *John Lloyd,* who married *Margaret,* sister of *Sir Roger Kynaston,* and their son Humphrey, who assumed the surname of *Wynne,* of Dyffryn, had a daughter *Katharine,* who married JOHN LLOYD Esq., of Dolobran.

27. **David,** (eldest son of Ivan Teg) of Dolobran, born 1523, was in Commission of the Peace for Montgomeryshire. He married first, EVA, daughter of EDWARD PRICE, Esq., of Eglusig, by whom he had no issue; and secondly, EVA, daughter of David Goch, Esq., by whom he had a son.

28. **David Lloyd,** of Dolobran, born 1549. He was also a Magistrate for Montgomeryshire. He married ALES, daughter of David Lloyd, Esq., of Llanarmonmynydd-maur, descended from Rivid Jharrd, Lord of Penllyn, and left a son

29. **John Lloyd,** of Dolobran, born 1575. He was in Commission of the Peace for Montgomeryshire. He resided in Coedeowrid. It is said "He lived in great state, wainscotted his parlors and halls, and was attended at Mivoid Church by twenty-four men, his tenants, with halberts, where he placed them in his great pew under the pulpit. He bought Owen

John Humphrey's estate, and presented to Myvoid Church most of the Communion plate." He married KATHARINE, daughter of Humphrey Wynn, Esq., of Daffryn, and left

30. **Charles Lloyd** of Dolobran, in Commission of the Peace for Montgomeryshire; born 1613; married ELIZABETH, daughter of Hon. Thomas Stanley, son of Sir Edward Stanley, son of Sir Foulk Stanley, son of Sir Piers Stanley, son of Sir Rowland Stanley, brother of LORD STRANGE, of Knuckyn—a branch of the Derby family.

31. **Charles Lloyd** (2d,) eldest son of CHARLES and ELIZABETH LLOYD of Dolobran, (who is treated more fully in connection with the English branch.) His brother (2) JOHN, born 1638, was one of the six Clerks-in-Chancery. He married JANE, only daughter of Sir Thomas Gresham, of Lidsey, in Surry, the thirteenth successive Knight of that family, and the munificent founder of the Royal Exchange. (3) ELIZABETH, born 1639, married Henry Parry, of Penamser, Merionetshire, and had issue. THOMAS, (3d son of Charles and Elizabeth Lloyd,) joined William Penn in the settlement of Pennsylvania, and whose descent I now purpose following.

AMERICAN BRANCH

OF THE

Lloyd Family.

31. **Thomas,** third son of CHARLES LLOYD and ELIZABETH (Stanley) his wife, was born 17 February, 1640. and died September 10, 1694.

He married (9th Sept. 1665) MARY, daughter of Colonel ROGER JONES. of Welsh Pool, who is said, by *Burke*, to have been Governor of Dublin, in the reign of James II, and defeated the Marquis of Ormond, in Ireland. This lady died in 1680, leaving heirs. from whom the American branch descend.

THOMAS LLOYD'S second wife was PATIENCE GARDINER. She died in Pennsylvania. leaving no heirs. (From Watson's Annals, p 449.) "*Friends' Meeting in Arch Street*, *Philadelphia*.—The first person ever interred in this ground was Gov. LLOYD's wife. She was a very pious woman. William Penn himself spoke at her grave— much commending her character. Because of his high estimation of her, and her excellent family. he offered, after her burial there. to give the whole lot to that family. Their descendants have ever since occupied the south-west corner, where Mrs. Lloyd was buried, as their exclusive ground."

Again— *From the Northern Monthly Magazine, January*, 1868:

"In the old Friends' burying ground of Philadelphia. may be seen the grave of Gov. Lloyd's wife, by the side of which William Penn stood and addressed the assembled mourners, years and years ago."

THOMAS LLOYD, joined William Penn in the colonization of Pennsylvania, and was Deputy Governor and President of Council in the Province, from 1684 to 1693. His children—Hannah, Rachel, Mordecai, John, Mary, Elizabeth, Margaret, Deborah and Samuel. (I purpose first following my especial branch.)

32. **Rachel,** daughter of Thomas and Mary Lloyd, was one of the three daughters who accompanied their father to America. She was born 1667, and married Samuel Preston, Mayor of Philadelphia, 1712. They left two daughters, viz:

　　MARGARET, born 1689, married Richard Moore 1709, and

33. **Hannah,** born 1693, married SAMUEL, eldest son of Samuel Carpenter, Penn's friend and associate, and died 1772.

　　Children of SAMUEL CARPENTER and HANNAH PRESTON, granddaughter of Gov. Thomas Lloyd:

　　1.　SAMUEL, married in Jamaica.
　　2.　RACHEL, died unmarried.
　　3.　PRESTON, married Hannah Smith.
　　4.　HANNAH, married Samuel Shoemaker.
　　5.　THOMAS, died unmarried.

34. **Preston Carpenter,** married HANNAH SMITH, of New Jersey.— Their children were:

　　1.　HANNAH, married Charles Ellet.
　　2.　SAMUEL.
　　3.　ELIZABETH, married Ezra Firth.
　　4.　RACHEL and JOHN died young.
　　5.　MARY.
　　6.　THOMAS, married Mary Tonkins.
　　7.　WILLIAM, married Elizabeth Wyatt. 2d. Mary Redman.

8. MARGARET, married James M. Woodnutt.

9. MARTHA, married Joseph Reeves.

35. **Hannah Carpenter** married CHARLES ELLET, of New Jersey.—
Their children were:

1. JOHN, married Mary Smith, of New Jersey.

2. SARAH, married Joseph Reeves, of New Jersey.

3. CHARLES, married Mary Israel, of Philadelphia.

4. WILLIAM, married Elizabeth Taggert, of New Jersey.

5. RACHEL CARPENTER, married James Wainwright, of Maryland.

6. MARY.

36. **John Ellet,** [eldest son of Charles Ellet, and Hannah Carpenter,
his wife,] married MARY SMITH, of Salem County, N. J.   Their
children were:

1. HANNAH CARPENTER ELLET, daughter of John and Mary Ellet,
married GEORGE WISHART SMITH, of Virginia.

2. MARIA CHAMLESS ELLET.

JOHN ELLET married, secondly, Sarah English, by whom he
had Henry T., Sarah E., John, and Joseph R. Henry T. alone leaving heirs, viz:—Jane, Joseph, Kate, Henry, John.

37. **Hannah Carpenter Ellet** married GEORGE WISHART SMITH, of
Virginia.   Their children

1. MARY ELLET SMITH, married Gen. Richard Thomas, of Talbot
Co., Maryland.   Their daughter, ANNA FRANCES.

2. MARGARET W. died young.

3. CHARLES PERRIN SMITH.

4. GEORGIANA WISHART SMITH, married Col. Samuel C. Harbert, of Philadelphia. Children Mary V. and Ella M.

HANNAH CARPENTER SMITH, married [secondly,] Joseph F. Brown, Esq.; of Salem, N. J., who left two sons—William Henry, [who has heirs,] and Joseph Francis, deceased.

38. **Charles Perrin Smith**, son of GEORGE W. and HANNAH CARPENTER SMITH, was born in Philadelphia. Married HESTER A. DRIVER, daughter of Col. MATTHEW DRIVER, of Caroline County, Maryland. Their children:

1. ELLEN WISHART, died 1858, aged 12 years.
2. CHARLES PERRIN, died 1864, aged 16 years.
3. ELIZABETH ALFORD SMITH.
4. FLORENCE BURMAN SMITH.

THE
Lloyd Family.
IN AMERICA.

Descendants of Governor Thomas Lloyd.

(CONTINUED.)

1. **Hannah,** born 1666, married first, JOHN DELAVAL, of Philadelphia; and secondly. RICHARD HILL, Mayor of Philadelphia 1710, 1715,'16, '17. By the latter she had five children, all of whom died unmarried.

2. **Rachel,** born 1667, married SAMUEL PRESTON, Mayor of Philadelphia, 1712. She left two daughters:

    1. MARGARET, born 1689, married 1709 Richard Moore, and had issue—Samuel who married Hannah Hill, Thomas, Rachel, Mordecai, who married Elizabeth Coleman 1793, Thomas married S. Emlen, Richard married Mary West; Thomas and Charles, twins,—Charles married Mileah M. Hill.

    2. HANNAH born 1693, married Samuel Carpenter, Jr., 1711, and had, 1 Samuel, married in Jamaica, 2 Rachel, unmarried, 3 Preston, who married Hannah Smith; [*the descent will be found in the Carpenter branch of this volume.*] 4 Hannah, married Samuel Shoemaker, had a son Benjamin, who married Elizabeth Warner,

and had a daughter Ann, married first, to Robert Morris, son of Robert Morris the Financier, and secondly to Francis Bloodgood.—5. THOMAS, unmarried.

3. **Morberai,** born 1669 ; lost at sea.

4. **John,** born 1671 ; died in Jamaica, 1692.

5. **Mary,** born 1674 ; married ISAAC NORRIS. Speaker of Assembly, and Mayor of Philadelphia, 1725.   Children—1. MARY, married Thomas Griffiths ; her son Isaac married Sarah Fitzwater ; daughters Mary and Hannah unmarried.   2. HANNAH married Richard Harrison, and had Thomas, (married Frances Scull, and had Amelia, who married R. McClanachan,) and Mary, (who married Jonathan Mifflin,) and Hannah, (who married Charles Thomson, Secretary to Congress during the Revolution of 1776.)   Other [3] children died in infancy. The sixth, ISAAC, married Sarah Logan, died 1776, leaving daughter Mary, who married John Dickinson, Governor of Delaware, and left two daughters—Sarah Norris, and Maria, who married Albanus Logan. 7. ELIZABETH. 8. DEBORAH. 9. THOMAS. 10. JOHN. 11. PRUDENCE. [died young.] 12. CHARLES, born 1712, married Margaret Rodman, and secondly, Mary Parker. 13. MARGARET, [died young.] 14. SAMUEL, [unmarried.]

6. **Thomas,** born 1675—married SARAH YOUNG and had issue :

1. PETER, married Mary Masters. Their son Thomas, married Mary Lawrence. By second wife, had daughter Sarah.

2. MARY. [unmarried.]

3. THOMAS, married SUSANNA OWENS—had daughter Sarah, who married Gov. William Moore, whose children were : 1. Thomas L.

(married Sarah Stamper, whose daughter Eliza married Richard Will-
ing.) Robert C. Moore, Elizabeth Moore who married Count Barbe
Marbois, French Minister Plenipotentiary to the United States. [He
organized all the French Consulates in this country, was appointed by
Louis XVI. Superintendent of St. Domingo; was French Minister to
Germany, Director of the Treasury, and finally one of the King's
Ministers. He negotiated the cession of Louisiana to the United
States, and saw it carried into effect. He was made Count of the
Empire, and Chief Officer of the Legion of Honor by Napoleon. He
entered the Senate in 1813, and the next year voted for the re-
establishment of the Bourbon dynasty. Louis XVIII appointed
him Peer of France, and Honorary Counsellor of the University, and
made him President of the Court of Accounts. His daughter
became Duchess of Plaisance, to whom Edmund About refers in his
" *Greece and Greeks of the present day*," as the daughter of one of
Napoleon's Ministers; she had married into one of the greatest
families of the Empire; loved by Maria Louisa, whom she served as
Maid of Honor; admired by the Court for her beauty; esteemed by
the Emperor for her virtues; after having showed herself to the
whole East with her daughter, for whom she dreamed of nothing
less than a crown, she at length settled permanently in Athens, in
the strength of her age and character.] Susanna Moore, married
Thomas Wharton, and had Lloyd Wharton, Kearney Wharton,
Moore Wharton and Sally Wharton.

4. JOHN, son of Thomas Lloyd, died unmarried.

5. MORDECAI married Hannah Fishbourne, and had a daughter,
Hannah, who married James Pemberton, and was mother of Rachel
Pemberton, who married Thomas Parke, M. D., and had Thomas,
James P., and Hannah.

7. CHARLES, unmarried.

7. **Elizabeth.**

8. **Margaret.**

9. **Deborah,** Born 1682—married M⸱ Moore, and left issue

    1. DEBORAH, married Dr. Richard Hill.

    2. HANNAH, died young.

    3. MARY, unmarried.

    4. HESTER.

    5. ELIZABETH.

    6. RACHEL.

DEBORAH, eldest daughter of Mordecai Moore, married Richard Hill, M. D., at South River, Maryland, 1757, had issue.

    1. RICHARD, unmarried.

    2. HANNAH, married Samuel Preston Moore, M. D., no issue.

    3. MARY, married Thomas Lamar.

    4. DEBORAH, died young.

    5. DEBORAH, married Richard Bisset, in Madeira.

    6. HARRIET, married John Scott.

    7. RACHEL, died young.

    8. HENRY, married Ann Meredith.

    9. RACHEL, married Richard Wells.

    10. MARGARET, married William Morris, and had issue.

    11. SARAH, married George Dillwyn.

    12. MILCAH M., married Charles Moore, M. D.

The children of Richard and Rachel Wells, were Richard, died

young. Samuel, Mary, Gideon, Henry, Hannah. Richard and Robert, [twins.] Rachel. William, George.

Family of MARGARET MORRIS, DAUGHTER OF DEBORAH MOORE, AND DR. RICHARD HILL.

1. RICHARD and

2. JOHN, (twins.) John married Abigail Dorsey, and left heirs.

3. DEBORAH, married Benjamin Smith, and left heirs.

4. RICHARD, married Mary Mifflin, and left heirs.

5. MARY.

6. GULIELMA MARIA, born 1766, married John Smith, son, of John Smith and Hannah Logan. Their descendants are:

1. HENRY HILL.

2. MARGARET HILL, married to Samuel Hilles.

3. RICHARD, married Susanna Collins, and left heirs.

4. RACHEL, married George Stewardson, left heirs.

5. MILCAH MARTHA.

6. JOHN JAY, born June 16, 1798, married in New York, 1824, to Rachel C. Pearsall.

Their children are Lloyd Pearsall, Albanus, Elizabeth P., Robert P., Gulielma Maria, Horace, John, Margaret Hill.

7. MORRIS, married Caroline Smith.

10. **Samuel,** born in Pennsylvania, died young.

GOV. THOMAS LLOYD

Was descended from an ancient Welsh family, which held its patrimonial estates for more than a thousand years.

MERIC, or MEIRIG, the proprietor of "*Dolobran*," and other large estates, is said in the legendary history of KING ARTHUR, to have been one of the four Knights who bore golden shields before that renowned Monarch at the great festival of Caerleon,* where he was crowned A. D., 517.—*See Penny Cyclopædia, article on "Arthur."*

The descent of the Lloyds, according to *Burke*, is traced from MEIRIG to IVAN TEG, of Dolobran, who assumed the surname of LLOYD about the year 1176.

THOMAS LLOYD, the fifth in descent from IVAN TEG, was born at Dolobran, 1640. He and his elder brother, CHARLES, were educated at the University of Oxford, and became distinguished for superior ability and learning. The brothers early joined themselves to the society of Friends, (1662.) and became highly useful and eminent members thereof.

In 1665, THOMAS LLOYD married MARY, daughter of GILBERT JONES, Esq., of Welsh Pool, in Montgomeryshire. *In Burke's History of the "Landed Gentry of Great Britain,"* she is said to have been the daughter of Col. Roger Jones, Governor of Dublin; but this can scarcely be correct, since in *Land and Plowden's History of Ireland,* the name is given as Michael Jones.

THOMAS LLOYD and MARY, his wife, were the parents of ten children, all of whom, except the youngest, were born on the Dolobran Estate, in Wales.

---

*At the great gathering at Caerleon, in Montgomeryshire, "tributary Kings in scores attended KING ARTHUR." The King was mortally wounded at the battle of Camlan, 512. Caerleon is believed to have been the capital of ancient Wales.

In 1683, THOMAS LLOYD arrived in Pennsylvania. He came in the ship
"AMERICA," Captain JOSEPH WASEY. They had a passage of eight weeks, and
landed the 20th of June, 1683. The following year he was appointed
President of Council, which position he held until 1691, when he was
commissioned Governor of the Province. He died 10th of 7th mo., 1694, in
the fifty-fourth year of his age; as it is written, "honored and respected by
all who knew him."

"Charles and Thomas Lloyd, having joined themselves to George Fox,
were rewarded by the loss of their estates. They were highly educated, and
both had taken degrees at Oxford. CHARLES removed to Birmingham, and
became a great Iron Master, and he, or his sons, established in that city,
"*Lloyd's Bank*," which is still the prominent monied institution of Birmingham, and familiarly known there as "the Bank."

THOMAS LLOYD having joined WILLIAM PENN, in the settlement of Penn-
sylvania, was at once regarded as one of the best and most useful of the
Colonists. His descendants are numerous and respectable. One daughter-
MARY, married ISAAC NORRIS, 7th of March, 1693–4. She died in the
"Slate-Roof House," O. S., 1748. Her obituary in *Franklin's Gazette* records:

" On the first of this month departed this life, Mrs. MARY NORRIS, relict of
ISAAC NORRIS, dec., late of Fairhill, and daughter of THOMAS LLOYD, Governor,
of this Province, in the 75th year of her age;—a gentlewoman remarkable
for her acts of charity, and which she endeavored so to conceal, as if she held
them a crime to make them public. She was an affectionate and obliging
wife, a tender mother, and a good mistress; a kind and consistent friend, and
generous and candid in her sentiments of persons of all denominations, was
truly beloved, and is universally lamented by all her acquaintances."

Another daughter, (RACHEL,) married SAMUEL PRESTON, and was the
mother of HANNAH, wife of SAMUEL CARPENTER 2d.

(I find the following reference to THOMAS LLOYD, in my MSS. mem. of the Carpenter Family:)

THOMAS LLOYD, the father of Rachel Preston, for some time Deputy Governor of Pennsylvania, was the son of CHARLES LLOYD, a gentleman of rank and fortune, and of ancient family and estate, called "Dolobran," in Montgomeryshire, North Wales. THOMAS LLOYD, was educated at the University of Oxford, and is represented as possessing superior attainments joined with great benevolence and activity of character. He died in Philadelphia, 1694, aged 51 years. His wife's name was MARY JONES, daughter of GILBERT JONES, Esq., of Montgomeryshire, North Wales, 1665.

WATSON, in his *Annals of Philadelphia*, says: "Having established his colony on the broad principles of Christian charity, and constitutional freedom, he, (Penn,) left the executive power in the hands of the Council, under the Presidency of THOMAS LLOYD, an eminent Quaker. Penn was absent about fifteen years." (Governor Lloyd resided in America about eleven years.

From "Bowden's History of Friends in America."

THOMAS LLOYD

Was born in North Wales about the year 1640. His father was possessed of considerable wealth, and descended from an ancient family in Dolobran, in Montgomeryshire. Thomas was the third son. After receiving an education in the best schools of the day, he was sent to the University at Oxford, where he is said to have made considerable proficiency in learning, and being a man endowed with good natural abilities, and much sweetness of disposition, he gained the notice and esteem of persons of the highest standing in society, and enjoyed opportunities of worldly advancement. In early life, however, his mind was richly visited from the Day Spring on High, humbling and contriting his soul, and giving him to see the emptiness of all things worldly in comparison of the riches of Christ his Saviour. Having heard of the people called Quakers, he went to hear them; where the Divine Power that pervaded the meeting humbled and bowed his spirit before the Lord: and clearly perceiving that their doctrines harmonized with those of the New Testament, he took up the Cross, and boldly professed them

before his fellow men. Having received a call to the Ministry, he became an eminent instrument in the hand of the Lord in turning many souls to righteousness; and in controversy with the learned, he proved a powerful advocate for the principles he professed. In common with many others of the Principality of Wales, he removed to Pennsylvania soon after its settlement as a Province, where he was of great service to that State in its infant days. In 1684 he was elected President of the Council, and in 1686 was one of the five appointed by Penn to the responsible office of "Council of State,"—an office he held until near the close of 1688, when he was released from its cares at his own express desire. In 1690, however, being again prevailed upon to exercise his talents in the civil offices of the country, he presided a second time in the Council, and in 1691, when the Council of State was superseded by the appointment of a Deputy Governor, he was chosen for this high office, which he held for about two years, until the appointment of Fletcher by the Crown of England. Although Thomas Lloyd, from his first arrival in Pennsylvania, took an active and conspicuous part in the civil affairs, it was nevertheless contrary to his own natural inclination, and so far from deriving any pecuniary advantage from devoting so much time and superior talents to the affairs of the Colony, it is asserted that his temporal interests suffered in consequence.

Again:

"Events having called WILLIAM PENN to his native land, it became needful for him to make some provision for the exercise of the Executive in his absence. For this purpose he authorized in the sixth month, 1684, the Provisional Council to to act in his stead, of which THOMAS LLOYD, mentioned in the last chapter, a Friend, highly qualified for the office, was made President. But the power of the government being committed to so many individuals, was attended with inconvenience, and in 1686 the Commission was entrusted to five persons, who were designated as "Commissioners of State." The parties chosen for this responsible office were all "Friends" of ability and high standing, including THOMAS LLOYD, who acted as Chairman. This arrangement continued until 1689, when, on the withdrawal of THOMAS LLOYD from the turmoils of office, and no Colonist being found suitable to succeed him, WILLIAM PENN appointed Capt. JOHN BLACKWELL, as his Deputy.

THOMAS LLOYD, named with such profound respect and ardent affection, by F. D. PASTORIUS, was Deputy Governor as long as he would serve;—a man of great worth, as a scholar and a religious man. He came to this country

in 1683, and died of a malignant fever 10th 7th month, 1694–5, leaving
behind him three daughters—very superior women, to wit:

RACHEL PRESTON,
HANNAH HILL,
MARY NORRIS.

His family were respectable, and ancient in Wales; he was himself
educated at the University; talked Latin fluently on shipboard with
PASTORIUS. He exercised as a public Minister among Friends in this country,
and in his own country suffered imprisonment for truth's sake.—*Watson's
Annals*, p. 518.

PASTORIUS dedicated a volume of acrostics and poems to his friends, the
three daughters of THOMAS LLOYD, commemorative of his and their safe
landing in Philadelphia. 20th 6mo., 1683. All his writings embrace much
of piety. These ladies he treats as eminently religious, to wit: RACHEL
PRESTON, HANNAH HILL, and MARY NORRIS,—each bearing the name of her
husband.

In the poem of the year 1715, he gives the name of the ship in which they
came, thus:

> "When I from Franckenland, and you from Wales, set forth—
> In order to exile ourselves towards the West;
> And there to serve the Lord in stillness, peace and rest;
>   A matter of eight weeks
> Restrained in a ship, "AMERICA" by name,
> Into America (*Am-rica* we came."
> (*Two Arabian words, meaning bitter and sweet.)

In his contributions of 26th, 6th month, 1718, to his lady friends and
shipmates, he commemorates their arrival as follows:

"The fortunate day of our arrival, although blessed with your good father's
company on shipboard, I was as glad to land from the vessel every whit as
St. Paul's shipmates were to land at Melito. Then Philadelphia consisted of
three or four little cottages, (belonging to Swedes,) and all the verdure being
only woods, and underwoods. among which I several times lost myself."—
Watson, p. 518.

Watson, p. 23, says:

" PENN had an excellent Deputy in THOMAS LLOYD, Esq., a scholar and a Christian. He always served reluctantly, and in 1688 resigned his place as Governor, but continued in the Council till his death, in 1694."

"WILLIAM PENN in his letter of 3d of 8th month, 1685, familiarly addressed him as " Dear THOMAS LLOYD," &c.—*Watson*, p. 43.

" In the course of his malevolent pamphleteering, KEITH had recourse to defamatory language, and, together with THOMAS BUDD, an active partizan, calumniated the character of SAMUEL JENNINGS as a Magistrate. In his anger, he had made some personal reflections upon THOMAS LLOYD, the Deputy Governor. The conduct of KEITH in assailing the integrity of these, and other civil officials of the Province, with a view to lessen them in the estimation of the Colonists, was an offence which the Magistrates considered ought not to be passed over in silence, especially as it was believed that his aim was to raise a public disturbance, and to furnish a pretext for subverting the government. In the sixth month, 1693, he was brought to trial, found guilty, and fined five pounds: but the fine, it appears, was not enforced, the object being simply to vindicate and uphold the authority of the government." —*Proud's History*, Vol. 1, p 376.

One of the early acts of the Provincial Legislature, after WILLIAM PENN's return to England, was the Proclamation of JAMES as King. The Proclamation was transmitted to the Home Government, of which the following is a copy from the original in the State Paper Office, Penna., B. T. Vol. 1:

" PHILADELPHIA, the 23d of the third month, (May,) 1685.

Pennsylvania.—The President and Members of the Provincial Council having received express advice this evening from the Proprietory and Governor of this Province and Territories, and transmitted to him from the Lords of the Council, of the decease of our late Sovereign CHARLES the Second, with speedy instructions to proclaim JAMES, Duke of York and Albany, and that his only brother and heir, KING JAMES, the Second. In obedience whereunto, we the President and Members of the Council, attended with the Magistrates, principal officers, and inhabitants of Philadelphia, doe unanimously proclaim JAMES, Duke of York and Albany, &c, by the decease of our late Sovereign, CHARLES the Second, to be our lawful liege Lord and King, JAMES the Second, of England, Scotland, France and Ireland, and among others of his dominions in America, of the Province of Pennsylvania and its territories, King. To whom we doe acknowledge faithful and constant obedi-

ence, with all hearty and humble affection. Beseeching God, by whom Kings
doth reign and Princes decree justice, to bless our present Sovereign King JAMES
the Second, with long, healthy, peaceable and happy years to reign over us.

God save King James the Second!

(Signed,)   THOS. LLOYD, President.

Dr. George W. Norris visited Dolobran a few years since. Traces of the residence of the Lloyds, Dolobran Hall, were then visible. The ancient grave yard
was turned into an orchard, through the turf of which memorial stones were seen.
—"*Hist. of Hill Family*," by JOHN JAY SMITH.

The Friends of HAVERFORD MEETING in Pennsylvania, recorded their affectionate
remembrance of THOMAS LLOYD's virtues in the following simple and antique but
beautiful tribute:

"He was by birth of them who are called the gentry, his father being a man of
considerable estate, and of great esteem in his time, of an ancient house and
estate called DOLOBRAN, in Montgomeryshire, Wales. He was brought up in the
most noted schools, and from thence went to one of the Universities, and because
of his superior natural and acquired parts, many of account in the world had an
eye of regard towards him. Being offered degrees and places of preferment, he
declined them all. The Lord beginning His work in him, and causing a measure
of His light to shine out of darkness in his heart, which gave him a sight of the
vain forms, customs and traditions of the schools and colleges, and hearing of a
poor despised people called Quakers, he went to hear them, and the Lord's power
reached unto him and came over him to the humbling and bowing of his heart and
spirits; so that he was convinced of God's everlasting truth, and received it in the
love of it, and made willing, like meek Moses, to choose rather to suffer affliction
with the people of the Lord, than the honors, preferments and riches of this world.
The earthly wisdom came to be of no reputation with him, but he became a fool,
both to it, and his former associates; and through self-denial, and taking up the
daily cross of JESUS CHRIST, which crucified his natural will, affections, and pleasures, he came to be a scholar in Christ's school, and learn the true wisdom which
is found from above. Thus, by departing from the vanities and iniquities of this
world, and following the leadings and instructions of the Divine Light, grace, and
spirit of Jesus Christ, he came more and more to have an understanding in the
mysteries of God's Kingdom, and was made an able Minister in the Everlasting
Gospel of Peace and Salvation; his acquired parts being sanctified to the services
of Truth.

His sound and effectual ministry, his great patience, temperance, humility and slowness to wrath, his love to the brethren, his godly care of the Church of Christ that all things might be kept sweet, savory, and in good order; his helping hand to the weak, and gentle admonitions, we are fully satisfied have a seal and witness in the hearts of all faithful Friends, who knew him both in the land of his nativity and these American parts. We may in truth say, he sought not himself nor the riches of this world, but his eye was to that which was everlasting, being given up to spend and be spent for truth and the sake of friends.

He never turned his back on the truth, nor was weary in his travels Sion-wards, but remained a sound pillar in the spiritual building. He had many disputes with the clergy, and some-called Peers, in England, and also suffered imprisonment, and much loss of outward substance, to the honor of truth, and stopping in a measure the mouths of gainsayers and persecutors. Yet these exercises and trials in the land of his nativity, which he sustained through the ability which God gave him, were small and not to be compared to the many and great exercises, griefs and sorrows he met withal and went through in Pennsylvania, from that miserable apostate George Keith, and his deluded company. Oh, the revilings, the great provocations, the bitter and wicked language, and rude behavior, which the Lord gave him patience to bear and overcome. He reviled not again, nor took any advantage; but loved his enemies, and prayed for them that despitefully abused him. His love to the Lord, his truth, and people, was sincere to the last. He was taken with a malignant fever the fifth of the seventh month, 1694, and though his bodily pain was great, he bore it with much patience. Not long before his departure, some friends being with him, he said: "Friends, I love you all; I am going from you, and I die in unity and love with all faithful Friends. I have fought a good fight, and kept the faith which stands not in the wisdom of words, but in the power of God. I have fought not for strife and contention, but for the grace of our Lord Jesus Christ, and the simplicity of the Gospel. I lay down my head in peace, and desire that you may all do so. Friends, farewell all." He further said to Griffith Owen, a Friend, then intending for England: "I desire thee to mind my love to Friends in England, if thou livest to get over to see them. I have lived in unity with them, and do end my days in unity with them, and desire the Lord to keep them all faithful to the end in the simplicity of the gospel." On the tenth day of the seventh month, being the sixth day of his sickness, it pleased the Lord to remove him from the many trials, temptations, sorrows and troubles of this world, to the Kingdom of everlasting Joy and Peace; but the remembrance of his innocent life and meek spirit lives with us, and his memorial is, and will remain to be sweet and comfortable to the faithful.

He was buried in Friends' burial ground, in Philadelphia, aged about fifty-five years, having been several years President and Deputy Governor of Pennsylvania."

For further particulars in reference to THOMAS LLOYD, see
Testimony of Dolobran Quarterly Meeting, 8 mo., 30, 1711.
Collection of MSS. Memorials, by John Smith, (in possession 1868, of John Jay Smith, Esq., Philadelphia Library.)
Epistle to Dolobran Quarterly Meeting, 6 mo., 2, 1684.—J. Smith's MSS.
Letter from John Humphreys to Charles Lloyd.
Testimony of James Dickinson, 1694.
Remarkable passages of his sufferings.
Richard Davies' account of remarkable circumstances, and also his account of the famous public dispute.
Short account of his last sayings.
"Piety promoted." 11, p. 202.
Mary Lloyd's address to her children.
Watson's Annals of Philadelphia.
Proud's History of Pennsylvania.
"Letters of Dr. Richard Hill, and his children; or, the History of a Family, as told by themselves." Collected and arranged by JOHN JAY SMITH. Privately printed for the descendants. 1 vol. octavo, portraits, p. p. 440, Philadelphia, 1854.

SAMUEL PRESTON, RICHARD HILL, and ISAAC NORRIS, the sons-in-law of THOMAS LLOYD, were all men of distinction in their day. They are thus briefly sketched by PROUD, the Historian of Pennsylvania:

SAMUEL PRESTON,

Was for a long time, one of the Governor's Council, and Treasurer of the Province of Pennsylvania; which office he discharged with much honor and fidelity. He was a man of great integrity to what he believed was his duty; his conduct in life being very instructive, and his practice a continual series of good offices. He was a person of such remarkable benevolence and open disposition of mind, as rendered advice and reproof from him the more acceptable and serviceable; and being of a fair and clean character, good judgment, and suitable presence of mind, his usefulness in that capacity was the more extensive and successful. He was a very valuable member of society among his friends, the Quakers, undertaking and performing many difficult offices and social duties therein with great cheerfulness, alacrity and utility; and was highly esteemed by them as an Elder, who ruled well

in his social capacity, and was worthy of double honor. He died in September, 1743, aged about eighty years.

I find the following in my MSS. mem. of the CARPENTER FAMILY:

SAMUEL PRESTON, the father of HANNAH, wife of SAMUEL CARPENTER, (Jr.,) was a distinguished coadjutor of SAMUEL CARPENTER, the elder. He was a native of Pautuxent, in Maryland, and one of the Commissioners appointed by PENN to adjust the boundary between Pennsylvania and Maryland. He was born in 1665, and died 1743, aged seventy-nine years. He married RACHEL LLOYD, July 6, 1688. He was an elder in the Society of Friends, and appears to have been greatly valued and beloved. He was distinguished for his social character, frank, animated manners, kind disposition, and strict integrity.

His wife, RACHEL, was born 1667. SAMUEL PRESTON was Mayor of Philadelphia 1711-12. He was also one of the Council. He left no male heir. One of his daughters married DR. MOORE, of Maryland, and another, HANNAH, the eldest son of Samuel Carpenter, Sen. (*Logan MSS. p. 3-492.*)

From "*Bowden's Hist. of Friends in America.*

SAMUEL PRESTON, was born in Maryland, and after the settlement of Pennsylvania, resided in Sussex county, Delaware, which he represented in the Assembly in 1701. He subsequently became a member of the Philadelphia Monthly Meeting, and filled some of the highest stations in the government of the Province,—having been for a long time one of the Council, and also Treasurer of the Province. His first wife was RACHEL, daughter of Gov. THOMAS LLOYD, and his second, MARGARET, widow of JOSIAH LANGDALE. He is described as a man of great benevolence, of sound judgment, and much presence of mind; whose life was instructive to others, "and his practice a continued series of good offices." In a "testimony" issued by his Monthly Meeting, he is thus spoken of: "He was an elder circumspect in his conduct, and carefully concerned for the good of the Church; active and serviceable in the maintenance of our Christian discipline; and by his attention to the dictates of Divine Grace, became well qualified for this service. He died in great resignation of mind, in 1743. in the seventy-ninth year of his age.

MARGARET PRESTON, wife of JOSIAH LANGDALE, was from Yorkshire.— She came to America in 1721, on a religious visit. In 1723 she repeated her visit to this country, and settled in Pennsylvania. Her husband died on the passage. She subsequently married SAMUEL PRESTON, of Philadelpoia. She travelled much in the work of the Ministry on the continent of North America.—her communications being "lively, sound and edifying." She died in 1742, in the 58th year of her age.—*Bowden's History.*

RICHARD HILL

Was born in Maryland, brought up to the sea, and afterwards settled in Philadelphia, having there married the widow of John Delavall, HANNAH, eldest daughter of the late Governor LLOYD, a woman of an excellent character, and very much esteemed and beloved. He was twenty-five years a member of the Governor's Council, divers times Speaker of Assembly, held several offices of trust, was for several years first Commissioner of Property, and during the last ten years of his life one of the Provincial Judges. His services in the religious society of Friends, the Quakers, of which he was for many years an active member, are said likewise to have been very considerable. He had by nature and acquisition such consistent firmness, as furnished him with undaunted resolution to execute whatever he undertook. His sound judgment, his great esteem for the English constitution and laws, his tenderness for the liberty of the subject, and his zeal for preserving the reputable order established in his own religious community, with his great generosity to proper objects, qualified him for the greatest services in every station in which he was engaged, and rendered him of very great and uncommon value in the place where he lived. He died in Philadelphia, 1729."—(Bowden's Hist of Friends.)

HANNAH HILL was the wife of Richard Hill, of Philadelphia, and relict of JOHN DELAVALL, her first husband. She was the daughter of Gov. THOMAS LLOYD, and born in Wales, at Dolobran, the family seat, in 1666. Her natural accomplishments were many, and she was conspicuous for her Christian virtues. It pleased the Lord to call her in her younger years to bear a public testimony to His truth, and though her communications were not long, yet "her doctrine dropped as the dew, and distilled as the small rain." She travelled in the service of the Gospel in New England, and other parts of North America, and for some years filled the office of Clerk to Womans' Yearly Meeting. "She was," says her friends, "a true servant of the Church, and in the sense of the Apostles' expressions, "one that washed the Saints feet," receiving into her house the Ministers and Messengers of the Gospel, for whom her love was great. During the latter years of her life much bodily weakness attended her, but under this she experienced the everlasting Arm to be near her, comforting and sustaining her in the eventide of life. She died in 1726, in the 61st year of her age."—Bowden's Hist. of Friends.

ISAAC NORRIS,

Of Philadelphia. He held many public offices with great reputation and honor: and his services in the affairs of his own religious community entitled him to very high and uncommon esteem among his friends, the Quakers, in which he was a principal person, and a good officer. He is said to have been endowed with great natural abilities, which he improved, and applied to the benefit of mankind, as a man truly sensible that one of the chief ends of man's existence is to be useful and beneficent to the human race, which he showed by his uniform conduct; and that to answer this end, men are to be taken as they are, and their lesser failings to be endured where they cannot be amended. The utility of his great talents was manifested by a prudent and consistent conduct in which he the more effectually succeeded and excelled, and that agreeable to duty and a good conscience, by constantly cherishing a temper and disposition of mind which overlooks or passes by the many dislikes, deficiencies and ungrateful things which are so commonly incident to mankind; so that by preserving through life a Christian moderation, and an even hand, he was on all occasions qualified to use and exert his abilities to more advantage. His example in this was noble and conspicuous, and his character in most respects so honorable among men in general, and his conduct so universally beneficial, especially to those of his own religious community, that he was an ornament to his country and profession, and his death a great loss to both, which was in the year 1735, while he was Chief Justice of Pennsylvania."—*Proud's Hist. Pa.*

ISAAC NORRIS emigrated from Jamaica, where he had been a merchant of respectable standing. In 1701 we find him a member of the Assembly of Pennsylvania, and during the remainder of his life he held many public offices "with great reputation and honor." He was endowed with good natural abilities, which from conscientious conviction "he improved and applied to the benefit of mankind." His services among Friends were many, and highly esteemed by them.—*From Bowden's History of Friends.*

The following anecdote illustrates the character of two of Gov. Lloyd's sons-in-law:

"At the instance of Gov. Evans, a Fort had been erected by the Territories at New Castle, avowedly for the protection of the river, but really, as the Provincialists inferred from its use, to vex the trade of the Province. All vessels navigating the Delaware were compelled to report themselves under a penalty of five pounds, and

a specific sum for every gun forced to bring them to. Inward bound vessels, not owned by residents, were subjected to the duty of a half pound of powder per ton of the capacity of the vessel. The Provincialists remonstrated against this abuse in vain. At length RICHARD HILL, WILLIAM FISHBOURNE and SAMUEL PRESTON, Quakers, distinguished for their private character and public services, resolved to resist the imposition. They embarked on board a vessel, dropped down the river, and anchored above the Fort. FISHBOURNE and PRESTON went ashore, and informed French, the Commander, that their vessel was regularly cleared, and demanded that they might pass uninterruptedly. This being refused, HILL, who had been used to the sea, stood at the helm, and passed the Fort with no other damage than a shot through the mainsail. French pursued in an armed boat, was alone taken on board, and the boat cut from the vessel, falling astern, he was led prisoner to the cabin : who now seeing his situation, pleaded his indisposition of body, upon which HILL asked him "if that really was the case, why did he come aboard?" LORD CORNBURY, Governor of New Jersey, and, as such, claiming to be Vice Admiral of the Delaware Bay, happened at that time to be at Salem, a little lower down on the Jersey side of the river; to him the prisoner was brought to give an account of his conduct. In this place, after French in a coarse manner, had been sufficiently reprimanded by LORD CORNBURY, upon a suitable submission and promise made, he was at length dismissed, but not without marks of derision from some of the attendants. This put a finishing stroke to these proceedings at the Fort of New Castle."—*Proud's History of Pa.*

THE
Lloyd Family
IN GREAT BRITAIN.

CHARLES LLOYD,
ELDEST BROTHER OF THOMAS LLOYD.

From "*An Account of the Travels, Services, &c., of that ancient servant of the Lord, RICHARD DAVIES,*' published in 1710. "In this book is an account of the persecution suffered by Mr. LLOYD, Mr. THOMAS LLOYD, his brother, and others."

"In the beginning of the year 1682, my dear friend CHARLES LLOYD and I went to visit Friends in Hertfordshire, Worcestershire, &c., and came through their meetings to London, before the Yearly Meeting. I acquainted my friends, GEORGE WHITEHEAD and WILLIAM PENN that I intended to go to Lord HYDE to acknowledge his kindness for his letter in my behalf to Bishop LLOYD. GEORGE WHITEHEAD said there was some service to be done for our suffering friends in Bristol, and it was thought convenient that three of the city and three of the country should go with the account of said sufferings, and desire the kindness of Lord HYDE to present them to the King. The three Friends for the country were CHARLES LLOYD, THOMAS WYNN and myself; for the city GEORGE WHITEHEAD, ALEXANDER PARKER, and one more. Our friend GEORGE WHITEHEAD told me that Sir LIONEL JENKINS, Secretary of State, was so cross and ill-humored that when the King was inclined to moderation and tenderness to suffering Friends, he often stopped and hindered the relief intended them. When we went to Whitehall, we waited a long time before we could speak with them, they being on a committee a considerable time; but we had sent in by the doorkeeper to acquaint Lord HYDE that we were there, and in time they sent for us in. The Secretary looked grim upon us. I went to Lord HYDE and acknowledged his kindness for his letter in my behalf to the Bishop. He told me I should inform the Bishop there should be liberty of conscience in England. I told him I did say so, and believed it would be so in God's time. Secretary JENKINS spoke in a scornful manner, and asked me what was Welsh for Quaker? I answered him "*Crynur Crynwyr,* it being the singular and plural number." But the Secretary said we had no Welsh for it, for there were no

Quakers in the Romans' days. My friend CHARLES LLOYD answered: "If thou didst ask my friend the question aright, he has answered thee right, for there is English, Welsh, Latin, Greek and Hebrew for Quaker." So the Secretary said: "Sir, I understand Welsh pretty well, and English and Latin and Greek, but if you go to your Hebrew, I know not what to say to you." I left my friend CHARLES LLOYD to engage with this peevish countryman, and presented Lord HYDE with a long list of names of men, women and children in the several prisons at Bristol. I desired him to be so kind as to present their sufferings to the King, which he said he would, and our friend GEORGE WHITEHEAD spoke further to him. Then I turned to the Secretary, who directed his words to me, and spoke to me thus, in Welsh:

"*Ma, yn ddrwg gennif, fod ru o Hiliogaeth yr hen Frittaniaid yrb rhai ydderbyniodd, y Grefydd Gristianogol yn gyntaf yd Loeger yn erbyn yr rhai sydd gweddiderbyn y wir Gristianogol yn gyntaf yd Loeger yn erbyn yr rhai sydd gwedi derbyn y wir Gristianogol yr awr hon.*"

The English is thus:

"I am sorry that one of the stock of ancient Britons, who first received the Christian faith in England, should be against those who have received the true Christian faith in this day."

He continued, he was not against our friends, but said our friends gave their votes for the election of Parliament men that were against the King's interests. I told him it was our birthright, and we were freeholders and burgesses, to elect men qualified to serve both the King and country; but how they were corrupted when they came within these walls, I knew not. The Secretary would have engaged farther with me in dispute about religion. I told him he was an ancient man, and that we had been a long time there upon our business, and if he would be pleased to dismiss us then, and appoint what time we should some morning wait upon him, we would, if he pleased, spend an hour or two with him in discourse about religion. Upon which he took off his hat, and thanked me kindly for my civility, but we heard no more about the dispute. Upon the whole, our friend GEORGE WHITEHEAD told me, he was more moderate to Friends afterwards than he had been before. The number of prisoners in the list delivered to Lord HYDE to be presented to the King, amounted in both prisons, to one hundred and thirty-nine, of which there were eighteen aged women from sixty and upwards, and eight children. In the latter part of the list it was said: "Blessed are the merciful, for they shall obtain mercy."

Descent from Charles Lloyd and Elizabeth Stanley,

(HIS WIFE,) OF DOLOBRAN.

1. **Charles,** *(heir.)

2. **John,** born 1638; one of the six Clerks-in-Chancery. Married JANE, only daughter of Sir THOMAS GRESHAM, of Lidsey, in Surry, the thirteenth successive Knight of that family, and the munificent founder of the Royal Exchange. By this lady he had issue:—JOHN (died unmarried;) SAMUEL. one of the six Clerks-in Chancery, left one daughter, JANE, who died young. Dr. LLOYD, late Lord Bishop of Oxford, was one of his descendants.

3. **Thomas,** who came to America, and joined WILLIAM PENN in the settlement of Pennsylvania. (Descent given elsewhere.)

4. **Elizabeth,** born in 1639—married Henry Parry, and had issue.

---

* CHARLES LLOYD (heir of CHARLES LLOYD and ELIZABETH STANLEY, his wife,) was born 9th December, 1637. He attached himself in 1662 to GEORGE FOX, and his followers, the founders of the Society of Friends. The "Independents" were at that time the dominant party,—the Episcopal Establishment having been overthrown,—and the Friends were as much persecuted by them as they were after the Restoration. It was at this period that CHARLES LLOYD having conscientiously refused to take the oath of allegiance and supremacy on the accession of Charles II, (though a more loyal subject did not exist in the country,) was at the instigation of an envious neighbor, EDWARD LORD HERBERT, of Chesbury (who desired his estates,) subjected to great persecution and losses. His possessions were put under præmunire, his cattle sold, and his mansion at Dolobran partially destroyed. Although a Magistrate for Montgomeryshire, and in nomination for its Sheriffalty at the time, the penal and oppressive laws against Sectarians, (arising from the excesses of some,) were enforced against CHARLES LLOYD with unmitigated rigor. He was taken with seven other gentlemen, who had embraced Friends' doctrines to Welshpool Jail, and confined there until the Act of JAMES II, released all persons detained for religious opinions,—a period of ten years.

His daughter ELIZABETH married JOHN PEMBERTON, Esq., of Bennett's Hill, near Birmingham, at whose house CHARLES LLOYD died. He married first, the daughter of SAMPSON LORT, Esq., (1661) of Eastmore and Stackpole Court, Pembrokeshire, other of Sir JOHN LORT by OLIVE, his wife, daughter of Sir JOHN PHILLIPS, Bart. of Picton Castle, and MARY his wife, eldest daughter of Sir JOHN PERROTT Viceroy of Ireland, *temp.* Queen Elizabeth, natural son of Henry VIII.

CHARLES LLOYD, wedded secondly, (1686,) ANN LAWRENCE, of Lea, in the county of Hereford. By his first wife, [who died 1685,] he had issue—

1. **Charles,** (3) of Dolobran, born August 18, 1662, and died January 21, 1747. He married SARAH, daughter of AMBROSE CROWLEY, Esq. Her brother, Sir Ambrose Crowley, had issue, 1, Elizabeth, married 1724-5 to John, Tenth Lord St John of Beltshoe; and her brother, John Crowley had a daughter married 1756 to John, Earl of Ashburnham.

    CHILDREN OF CHARLES AND SARAH LLOYD:

    CHARLES, (4) born 1697: married JANE, daughter of Richard Wilkins, of Thornbury, and by her had 1. CHARLES EXTON, of Dolobran, (died in France 1773.) 2. JAMES, born 1743 (unmarried,) died 1787. He sold the Dolobran estates in 1789 bequeathed to him by his brother Charles Exton Lloyd. 3. JANE, born 1728, married Lewis Owen of Tythay Gareck, near Dollgelle, and had issue Owen, Charles, Humphrey and Jane who married John Lewis, Esq., of Haverford-west, and had several children,— one of whom, SARAH, married H. Knight, Esq., of London. 4. MARY, born 1730, and died 1753. 5. SARAH, born 1732, married Thomas Robinson, of Coventry—died 1816. 6. Elizabeth born 1734, married first Edward Evans, of Welshpool, and secondly Oliver Jones, of the same place. 7. HANNAH, born 1735, married Robert Perkins of London, and had daughter Jane Lloyd Perkins, who married Richard Harford, Esq., of Elbevale, near Bristol, and had issue. 8. PHEBE, born 1738, and 9. SUSANNA, born 1739.

2. SARAH, born 1694: married 1719, John England, Esq., of Bridgenorth, and had issue, John (unmarried,) Charles, married Sarah, daughter of John Gulson.

3. ELIZABETH, died young.

2. **Sampson,** (2nd son of CHARLES LLOYD, and nephew of Gov. THOMAS LLOYD, of Pennsylvania,) was born February 26, 1664; married first ELIZABETH, daughter of Sybill Good, Esq., and by her had

    1. ELIZABETH.

    2. SARAH, who married John Gulson, Esq., of Coventry, and had William, John, Anna, and Mary.

SAMPSON LLOYD, married secondly, MARY, daughter of AMBROSE CROWLEY, Esq. Their children,

    1. CHARLES, married Sarah, daughter of Benjamin Careless, Esq., and died 1741, leaving Charles; Benjamin, died 1804, (leaving daughter Sarah, who married William Brewin, and had son Charles, who married in 1832, Sophia, daughter of Samuel Galton, Esq., of Duddeston Hall, Warwickshire—a Banker of Birmingham.)

    2. AMBROSE, died 1742, leaving Anna, who married Alfred Lloyd, Esq., her cousin.

    3. SAMPSON, of whom presently.

The third son.

3. **Sampson Lloyd, Esq.,** a Banker of Birmingham, born May 15, 1699, married Sarah, daughter of Richard Parks, Esq., of Old Park, near Wednesbury, Staffordshire, and by her had

    1. SAMPSON, of BORDESLEY, born 1728, who married Rachel, daughter of Samuel Barnes, Esq., of London, and by her had Sampson, born 1765, married Hannah Harman, of London.

    2. SAMUEL, of BORDESLEY, in Warwickshire, a Banker in Birmingham, born 1768, married 1791, Rachel, daughter of George Braithwaite, Esq., of Kendal, in Westmorland, and had issue,—GEORGE BRAITHWAITE, Banker in Birmingham, born January 5, 1794, married Mary, daughter of Jesse P. Dearman, Esq., of Birmingham, and had issue, Sampson Samuel, (born 1820,) and George B., (born 1824.) SAMUEL, (George Braithwaite Lloyd's brother,) an iron-master at Wednesbury, born 1795, married Mary Honeychurch, of Falmouth, and had issue, Samuel, Joseph Foster, Wilson, Rachel Jane, Mary, Amy Elizabeth, Sarah.

WILLIAM, (brother of George B., and Samuel,) born 1798. He was a physician in Birmingham.

BARNES.

ISAAC, born 1801, married Mary, daughter of Isaac Rigge, Esq., of Kendal, and had issue—John Sanderson, Henry, and Edward.

THEODORE, born 1806, married Anna, widow of Cornelius Ash, Esq., of Bewdley, and had a son, Theodore.

SAMPSON.

WILSON.

DEBORAH, married George Stacy, Esq., of Tottenham, and had issue.

RACHEL, married Robert, son of Luke Howard, and had issue.

SARAH, married Alfred Fox, Esq., of Falmouth, and had issue.

3. DAVID, (brother of Sampson and Samuel of Bordesley,) was a banker at Hailsworth, in Suffolk, born 1769; first married Elizabeth, daughter of John Hanbury, Esq., of Coggeshall; secondly, to ————, daughter of ———— Day, Esq.

4. RICHARD, (brother of Sampson of Bordesley,) born 1772, married Elizabeth, daughter of J. Harmon, Esq., and had issue,—1. Richard H., (married Isabella Mary, daughter of William Borrodaile, Esq., of Balham, in Surry.) 2. Elizabeth Beatrice, (married Richard Alsager, Esq., M. P., for East Surry.) 3. Frances. 4. Charlotte, (who married Rev. G. Echalez, of Appleby.

5. ALFRED, a Banker in Birmingham, born 1780, married Anna, daughter of Ambrose Lloyd, Esq., and had issue,—Alfred, Edgar, Hubert, Ambrose, George, and Ellen.

6. HENRY, a Banker in London, born 1784.

7. GEORGE, born 1786, Captain in 3rd Light Dragoons, died 1832.

8. MARY, died 1816.

9. SARAH, married Joseph Foster, Esq., of Bromley House, Essex, and had issue.

10. RACHEL, married W. P. Summerfield, Esq., of Allesley, in Warwick-shire, and had issue.

11. ELIZABETH, married John Biddle, Esq., late of Neach Hill, Shropshire, now of Leamington, and has a daughter Rachel married to George Lloyd, M. D., of Albrighton.

12. ANNE, married W. P. Summerfield, Esq., and has with other issue, Sampson Summerfield, a banker in Shiffnal.

13. AGATHA, married Joseph Biddle, Esq., of Birmingham.

14. CHARLOTTE, married Thomas Phelps, Esq., of Dublin, and had a son, Joseph Lloyd Phelps.

15. CATHARINE, married George Birkbeck, F. R. S., a physician in London, and had a son, William Lloyd Birkbeck, barrister-at-law.

16. LUCY, died young.

Sampson Lloyd, married secondly, (Sept. 17, 1731,) Rachel, daughter of Nehemiah Champion, Esq., of Bristol, and had several children, who died in infancy, and then,

2. **Nehemiah,** born 1745, died 1801.

3. **Charles,** (of whom presently.)

4. **John,** Banker in London, born January 6, 1750, died 1811, married Elizabeth, daughter of Thomas Corbyn, Esq., of Laytonstone, Essex, merchant in London, and had issue:

CORBYN, Banker in London, married Emily, daughter of J. Atlee, Esq., of Wandsworth, and has three daughters—Emily, Rosaline and Bertha.

EDMUND, born 1787, died in Madeira.

AMBROSE, born 1789.

MARK, born 1790, Lieutenant in the Scots Greys.

LLEWELLYN, of Lapp Cottage, Dalecarlia, Sweden, author, &c., born 1792.

JOSEPH, of Lambeth, born 1796.

RACHEL.

LUCY, married Halsey Janson, Esq., of Stamford Hill, Middlesex, and has issue—Edward, Henry, Louisa, Mary Elizabeth, Emma, Clara, and Lucy Matilda.

ELIZABETH.

5. **Ambrose,** born 1754, died 1787, married Elizabeth, daughter of John Talwin, Esq., of Royston, in Herefordshire, and had a daughter Anna, married her cousin, Alfred Lloyd, Esq., of Goldicot House, Warwickshire, and has issue.

6. **Mary,** daughter of Sampson Lloyd, born 1736, died 1770, married Osgood Hanbury, Esq., of Holfield Grange, near Coggeshall, in Essex, and had issue.

JOHN OSGOOD HANBURY, born 1757, died 1773.

SAMPSON HANBURY.

OSGOOD HANBURY, of Holfield Grange, a Banker in London, born 1765, married Susannah Willet, daughter of John Barclay, Esq., Banker of London, and has issue : 1. Osgood, of Tulse Hill, Banker of London, born 1794, married Eleanor, daughter of W. Hall, Esq., and has two sons and two daughters. 2. Robert, of the firm of Truman, Hanbury, Buxton & Co., Brewers, in London, married and has issue. 3. Henry, born 1798. 4. Sampson. 5. Arthur, born 1801, Rector of Bewars. 6. Philip, a Banker in London, born 1802. 7. Susan, married Robert Field, Esq., and has issue, Anna. 8. Rachel, married Robert Barclay, Esq., of Clapham-son of Charles Barclay, Esq., M. P., and has issue, Mary.

CHARLES HANBURY, of Halsted, Essex, a Banker in Bury, Ipswich, born 1766, married daughter of John Bland, Esq., died 1825, leaving issue. of whom Priscilla, married W. P. Honeywood, Esq., M. P., for Kent.

RICHARD HANBURY, died young.

SAMPSON HANBURY, of Poles Hall, Herts, a brewer in London. (Truman, Hanbury, Buxton & Co.,) born 1769, died 1835, married Agatha, daughter of Richard Gurney, Esq., of Norwich, and sister of Hudson Gurney, Esq., of Keswick Hall, Norfolk, M. P. for Newton.

ANNA HANBURY, married 1782, Thomas Fowell Buxton, Esq., of Berkensted Hall, Hertfordshire, and had a son, Sir Thomas Fowell Buxton, M. P., for Weymouth.

RACHEL HANBURY, married Richard Gurney, Esq., M. P., for Norwich, and died 1825, leaving issue.

MARY HANBURY, born 1770, died 1826; married her cousin David Lloyd, Esq., of Kenilworth.

7 **Rachel,** married David Barclay, Esq, Brewer in London, (Barclay. Perkins & Co.,) died 1809.

Sampson Lloyd's second son by his second marriage,

Charles Lloyd, Esq., of Birmingham, born Aug. 22, 1748, inherited by bequest his brother Nehemiah's estates in Warwickshire. He married Mary, only daughter of James Farmer, Esq., of Bingley House, Birmingham, and by her (who, was born 1750, and died 1821,) had issue:

1. **Charles,** (heir.)

2. **Thomas,** of Bingley House, in Commission of the Peace, for the county of Warwick, born 1776, married 1802, Sarah, daughter of Francis Hart, Esq., of Nottingham, and has issue:

    1. FRANCIS, born 1803; high bailiff of Birmingham—1833, a magistrate for Warwickshire, and an officer in the County Yeomanry.

    2. JAMES, born 1806, a merchant in Gloster, married Elmira, daughter of J. Page, Esq.

    3. CHARLES, of Birmingham, born 1807.

    4. WILLIAM REYNOLDS, born 1808, a merchant at Gloster.

    5. NEHEMIAH, of Birmingham, born 1810.

    6. THOMAS, born 1814.

    7. PRISCILLA, born 1805.

3. **Robert,** born 1778, married Hannah, daughter of Francis Hart, Esq., of Nottingham, died 1811, leaving issue:

    1. ROBERT, born 1811.

    2. HANNAH, born 1805.

    3. MARY, married 1832, Rev. John Geddes Crosbie, of Fenwick Manse, in Ayrshire, and has issue:

      SARAH.

4. **Thomas,** a merchant in Birmingham, born 1779, married Susannah, daughter of John Whitehead, Esq., of Barford, Warwickshire, Banker, and by her left—

    ANNA, born 1806, Susan, born 1808, Agatha, [married George Esgstrom, Esq., a Swedish merchant in London.]

5. **Plumstead,** of London, born 1780, married first, Frances Isabella, daughter of J. Betenson, Esq., of Ipswich, and by her had—

Mary Elizabeth, [married her cousin, Edward Lloyd,] Emma, Isabella, [married Henry Russell, Esq., of Toronto, Canada.]

PLUMSTEAD LLOYD, married secondly, Jane, daughter of John Howell, Esq., and has by her a daughter, Jane Howell.

6. **Priscilla,** married Rev. Christopher Wordsworth, D. D., formerly Dean of Bocking, and present Master of Trinity College, Cambridge, author of Ecclesiastical Biography, &c., brother of William Wordsworth the poet, and has issue:

    1. John Wordsworth, born 1805, Fellow of Trinity College, Cambridge, 2. Charles Wordsworth, Scholar of Christ Church, Oxford, second Master of Winchester College, born 1806, married Charlotte, daughter of Rev. J. Day. 3. Christopher Wordsworth, Fellow of Trinity College, Cambridge, late Public Orator of the University, and head Master of Harrow, born 1807.

7. **Olivia,** married Paul Moon James, Esq., of Wake Green, Worcestershire, Magistrate, a Banker in Birmingham, and High Bailiff, 1834.

8. **Mary,** married George Braithwaite, Esq., of Kendal, died 1822, leaving issue: George, born 1810; Thomas, born 1816; Samuel, born 1820; James, 1820; Mary, [married Alfred Hingeston, Esq., M. D., of Plymouth;] Deborah.

9. **Anna,** married Isaac Braithwaite, Esq., of Kendal, and has issue: Isaac, born 1810; Charles Lloyd, 1811; George Foster, 1813; Robert, 1816; Joseph B., 1818; Anna and Caroline.

10. **Caroline,**

11. **Agatha,** married James Pearson. Esq., a Banker in Birmingham, and has issue.

*CHARLES LLOYD, Esq., [heir,] of Birmingham, in the county of Warwick, born February 12, 1775, married April 24, 1799, SOPHIA, daughter of Samuel Pemberton, Esq., of Birmingham, and has issue:

    1. CHARLES GROSVENOR, born 1800.

2. JAMES FARMER, born 1801, married Juliana, daughter of ————— Ormsby, Esq., and has with a daughter, a son, Charles Arthur, born at Versailles, April 2, 1834.

3. OWEN, born 1803, M. A., in holy orders, Curate of Ambleside, and Vicar of Langdale, Westmorland.

4. EDWARD, born 1804, married Mary Elizabeth, daughter of Plumstead Lloyd, Esq.

5. ARTHUR, born 1807.

6. MARY SOPHIA, married William Thompson, Esq., of Leamington, and has a daughter, Sarah Sophia.

7. PRISCILLA, married Charles Romain Millett, of Versailles, and has a daughter, Sophia.

8. AGATHA, married Ernest Camille du Vallon, Captain in 8th French Dragoons, and has issue.

9. LOUISA.

CHARLES LLOYD, died January 16, 1828, and was succeeded by his eldest son, CHARLES LLOYD.

Addenda.

SIR THOMAS FOWELL BUXTON, M. P., a British Legislator and philanthropist, was the son of Thomas Fowell Buxton, Esq., of Barkenstead Hall, and Anna Hanbury, his wife. He was born April 1, 1786, at Castle Hedingham, Essex, and died at his residence near Aylsham, February 19, 1845. According to the "*New American Cyclopædia,*" he was educated at Donnybrook, and Trinity College, Dublin. At the age of twenty-one he married Miss Gurney, and became brother-in-law to Mrs. Elizabeth Fry. The sufferings of the poor inhabitants of Spital-fields were so apparent to him, that in 1816 he took an active part in collecting £44,000 for their relief. Prison discipline also interested him and in conjunction with Mrs. Fry, and Mr. Hoare, his brother-in-law, he personally examined into the state of British prisons, and published the result of his inquiry. From this came the Prison Discipline Society, which led to the removal of many evils. From 1818 to 1837, he was Member of Parliament for Weymouth. For a period of nearly twenty years, he was constant in his attendance, and a frequent speaker. Prison discipline, the amelioration of the criminal law, the suppression of lotteries, the abolition of Hindoo widow burning, and of slavery, were subjects on which he was always earnest, and sometimes eloquent. He cordially co-operated with Mr. Wilberforce on the anti-slavery question, and succeeded him as the recognized Parliamentary leader of the party: Brougham, Lushington, Macauley, Mackintosh and other liberals, strongly supporting him. He was a member of the Parliament which in 1833, abolished Colonial slavery: voting £20,000,000 to compensate the slave owners. After he left Parliament, he published a book against the African slave trade. His last active part in public business was to participate in a meeting held at Exeter Hall, in 1840, under the presidency of Prince Albert, which led to the expedition to the Niger in the following year.

CARPENTER FAMILY.

THE persecution of Friends in England commenced about the year 1648, and reached its height during the reign of CHARLES II. when the prisons were filled with victims, without regard to sex, age or condition, and ship-loads were banished from the kingdom. The large accession of an industrious and thrifty population to the island of Barbadoes, through this cause, speedily developed its natural resources, and induced others voluntarily to repair thither. Among them, it is believed, was SAMUEL CARPENTER. The time of his arrival can only be conjectured. He was born in 1650, fifteen years prior to the general banishment of 1664-5. According to *Besse*, in 1673 he suffered [in Barbadoes] considerably in distraints for refusing to bear arms. He had then reached his twenty-third year; and it is quite probable that this difficulty with the authorities occurred soon after his arrival. The opinion that he voluntarily repaired to Barbadoes, is fortified by the circum-stance of his possessing ample wealth; for had he been proscribed [as in the case of CHARLES LLOYD, and others,] his property, most likely, would have been placed under praemunire.* It is a matter of history that "many Friends accumulated great wealth, with which came influence and social position. They became not unfrequently the associates and rivals of nobles and statesmen: they found themselves in great assemblies, sitting at the side of dignitaries of the Church, who had seats in the House of Lords, and par-ticipated in national legislation. Their property was in real estate, or such personal effects as attracted the eye of the tax-gatherers, and easily subjected to distraint. The Friends by their principles were bound to resist the pay-

* Introducing or acknowledging a higher power in the land, and creating *imperium in imperio*, by paying that obedience to Papal authority which belonged to the King. It was charged that Friends acknowledged allegiance to spiritual convictions rather than Kingly authority. The penalty placed the offender out of the King's protection, his possessions were forfeited to the King, and his body remained in prison at the King's pleasure, or during life.

ment of tithes, and the performance of military duty, and did so to the damage of their worldly estates, and too often, personal liberty."

SAMUEL CARPENTER joined WILLIAM PENN, in Philadelphia, 1682, where, in addition to many responsible official duties, he engaged largely in foreign commerce. He died at his original mansion,* in King [now Water] street, April 10, 1714, in the 64th year of his age.

SAMUEL CARPENTER is referred to in terms of regard by WILLIAM PENN in a letter addressed in 1684, to THOMAS LLOYD, President of Council of State. He was one of the Trustees of Public Schools established by Friends in Philadelphia in 1689, and also a Member of the Provincial Assembly. In 1701 PENN appointed him Member of the Council of State. He appears to have been constantly employed with public affairs, either as Member of the General Assembly, Council of State, or Treasurer of the Province. The following notice of his death is taken from "*Proud's History of Pennsylvania:*"

"In the year 1714 died SAMUEL CARPENTER, the Treasurer of the Province, who was succeeded in office by SAMUEL PRESTON. SAMUEL CARPENTER arrived early in the Province, and was one of the most considerable traders and settlers of Pennsylvania, where he held for many years some of the greatest offices in the government, and throughout great variety of business preserved the love and esteem of a large and extensive acquaintance. His great abilities, activity, and benevolent disposition of mind in divers capacities, but more particularly among the "Friends", are said to have rendered him a very useful and valuable member, not only of that religious society, but also of the community in general."

"SAMUEL CARPENTER, one of the early settlers of Pennsylvania, and for a long period the most prominent among the merchants of Philadelphia, departed this life in the year 1713, [1714.] He occupied some of the most important posts in the civil government, being a Member of the Governor's Council and Treasurer of the Province. "Through a great variety of business he preserved the love and esteem of an extensive acquaintance. His abilities, activity and benevolence rendered him a useful and valued member of both civil and religious society."—*Janney's History of Friends.*

* This house was subsequently occupied by his son Samuel.

Watson, the Historian, says:

"The name of Samuel Carpenter is connected with everything of a public nature in the early annals of Pennsylvania. I have seen his name at every turn in searching the old records. He was the Stephen Girard of his day in wealth, and the William Sansom in the improvements he suggested, and edifices which he built."

"My Mss. Book of Annals of Philadelphia thus reads, p 162: "Samuel Carpenter was one of the greatest improvers and builders in Philadelphia, and, after William Penn, [about 1700,] the wealthiest man in the Province."

There is no way of ascertaining the extent of his possessions; but the following items are incidentally alluded to in *Watson's Annals:*

1. A large property now covered by the town of Bristol, Pa., with extensive Saw and Grist Mills.

2. The "Slate Roof House" on Second Street, Philadelphia. Gov. Penn resided in this house in 1700, and it was afterwards owned by William Trent, the founder of Trenton. John, the eldest son of William Penn, was born here. In 1696 the Assembly of the Province met in this house. It was subsequently occupied by the officers of 424 Highlanders, and also by those of the Royal Irish. Baron de Kalb, who fell at the battle of Camden, S. C., during the Revolution, was an inmate. Gov. Forbes, the associate of Gen. Braddock, died here. In 1868 the old mansion was demolished, and its site occupied by the Commercial Exchange.

3. Certain Lots on the north side of Market Street, Philadelphia, and reaching halfway to Arch, bounded at extremities by the Delaware River and Wood Street.

4. He was joint proprietor with William Penn of a Grist Mill on the site of Chester—the third Mill in the Province.

5. A Lot extending from the river to Second Street, and from Norris Alley to Walnut.

6. A Crane, Bakery, and Mansion House on the wharf. Also a store house and grocery, and a Tavern called the "*Globe.*"

7. Half of a Mill at Darby, and a Saw Mill, with a pond, covering 300 acres.

8. Five thousand acres in Poquassing Creek, 15 miles from Philadelphia.

9. The Island in Delaware River opposite Bristol—350 acres.

10. An Estate of 350 acres called "Sepviser Plantation," a part of Fairhill, at the north end of Philadelphia.

11. 1000 acres of land in Pilesgrove, Salem County, N. J., part of which he sold in 1700 to John Wood.

12. Fifty acres in New Jersey, opposite Philadelphia.

13. 600 acres in New Jersey, on the river, bounded in part by South Branch of Timber Creek.

14. Eleven hundred acres in Elsinborough, Salem County, N. J., situate near the Swede's Fort. The farm now owned by Clement Hall is part of this tract. The original purchase was made in 1696.

15. Three-sixteenths of five thousand acres of land, and a mine called Pickering's Mine.

16. A Coffee House (at or near Walnut and Front Street, Philadelphia,) and Seales.

He was actively engaged in foreign commerce, and owner in full or part of numerous vessels trading to the West Indies, and various parts of world.

On the 12th October, 1684, SAMUEL CARPENTER, sen., married HANNAH HARDIMAN, a native of Haverford-west, South Wales, Great Britain. She was born in 1646, and having joined the Society of Friends, emigrated to Pennsylvania, where she became a Minister of that persuasion. She died May 24, 1728, aged 82 years. A memoir of her character and services, published in *Bean's Collection of Memoirs,* speaks of her as a most exemplary woman.

"HANNAH CARPENTER was born in Haverford-west, South Wales, where she was convinced of the principles of Friends, and where, it is said, she became very serviceable to those who were in bonds for Christ's sake. After her settlement in Pennsylvania, she was united in marriage to SAMUEL CARPENTER, of Philadelphia, a Friend of considerable influence in the Province. Her Gospel Ministry was attended with much Divine sweetness, and was truly acceptable and edifying. She was a tender, nursing mother in the Church, and a bright example of Christian meekness. Her decease took place in 1728, at the advanced age of eighty two years."—*Bowden's History of Friends in America.*

In a letter written after SAMUEL CARPENTER's death to his daughter HANNAH, he is thus noticed by THOMAS STORY, a distinguished minister of that day:

"The Lord has gathered my dear friend to himself.   *   *   *   I am fully satisfied he has attained the state of the just and is praising his God, and our God, in the heavens, in joy unspeakable, which never changeth.'

James Logan, in a letter to William Penn, says:

"That worthy and benevolent man, SAMUEL CARPENTER, is to be interred to-morrow, after about two weeks illness. A fever and cough with rheumatic pains, carried him off. I always loved him, and his generous and benevolent disposition; so I find at his exit, few men could have left a greater degree of concern on my thoughts. I need say nothing to thee on the loss of such a man, but a sense of it was seen in the faces of hundreds. I am satisfied his humble and just soul is at rest."

The following tribute is from *Friend's Memorial*, written shortly after his decease:

"He was a pattern of humility, patience and self-denial; a man-fearing God, and hating covetousness; much given to hospitality and good works. He was a loving affectionate husband, tender father, and faithful friend and brother.   *   *   *   *   He was ever ready to help the poor, and such as were in distress. His memory is precious to the living, and renowned among the just: and though he is dead, yet he speaketh, and his name shall be recorded among the faithful for generations to come."

In the summer of 1712 Penn thus wrote to some of his friends in America:

"Now know, that though I have not actually sold my government to our truly good Queen, yet her able Lord Treasurer and I have agreed to it. But I have taken effective care that all the laws and privileges I have granted you shall be observed by the Queen's Governor, &c.; and that we who are Friends, shall be in a more particular manner regarded and treated by the Queen. So that you will not, I hope and believe, have a less interest in the Government, being humble and discreet in your conduct." [This letter was addressed to SAMUEL CARPENTER, EDWARD SHIPPEN, RICHARD HILL and others.]

The following extract from an article in *Philadelphia Commercial List*, published a few years since, speaks more particularly of SAMUEL CARPENTER, as a merchant:

SAMUEL CARPENTER.

The curious view of Philadelphia, by Peter Cooper, which hangs in the Philadelphia Library, and is supposed to have been painted about the year 1714, contains as a conspicuous object the store house of SAMUEL CARPENTER, situate upon the wharf below Chestnut street. "Carpenter's stairs," nearly opposite, was a passage from Front street to what was then called King street, but which since the Revolutionary war has been called Water street. Carpenter's wharf was a well-known land-mark among the drab coated men who came over with Penn, and Samuel Carpenter has literally the distinction of having been one of our *first* merchants. It is impossible, at this time, to give much information in relation to the state of our commerce during the period between the settlement of the city, in 1682, and the death of Samuel Carpenter, in 1714: but all accounts agree that Carpenter was

the most successful merchant of his time. Commerce was then mostly confined to costing trade, with greater voyages occasionally to the English West India Islands. Barbadoes and Jamaica were the principal points of intercourse, and from those islands came many of the settlers whose blood still courses through our Philadelphia families. Our exports were mostly agricultural products, in which grain, flour and tobacco held a large proportion. Skins and furs were important articles of trade also. Ships were then more plentiful than they are now, but these ships were small craft of from one hundred to two hundred tons burthen, there was much danger from pirates, even in the short voyages which those vessels made, and the names of Kidd and Blackbeard are yet remembered.

Samuel Carpenter writing, in 1708, to Jonathan Dickinson, says :—" I am glad thou didst not come this summer, for craft from Martinico and several other privateers have been on our coast, and captured many. Our vessels here have been detained some time in fear of the enemy, and now, by this conveyance to Jamaica, they are hurrying off sixteen vessels, to join convoy at the capes under the York man-of-war."

* * * * * * * * * * * * *

It must have been with regret that a merchant of so much ability and experience felt himself compelled to withdraw from active participation in trade. James Logan, in writing to the Proprietors of Pennsylvania concerning Samuel Carpenter says—" He lost by the war of 1703, because the profitable trade he before carried on almost entirely failed."

Isaac Norris, in a letter dated June 10, 1705, says of him—" That honest and valuable man, whose industry and improvements have been the stock whereon much of the labors and successes of this country have been grafted, is now weary of it all, and is resolved, I think prudently, to wind up and clear his encumbrances." He carried out his intentions, disposed of considerable portions of his property, and retiring to the Sepviva estate, which was near enough to the city to be of convenient access, devoted his leisure time exclusively to public affairs. In 1689 he was a Trustee for the Quaker School and a Member of the Assembly. In 1701 he was appointed a Member of the Provincial Council, the official advisers of the Governor. Subsequently he became the Treasurer of the Province, a position which he held at the time of his death, in 1714.

Whilst it is impossible to give much information concerning our early merchants, it is equally proper to make this record of the few items gleaned in relation to Samuel Carpenter. A member of the Society of Friends, and associate of the founder of the State, he entered into business immediately upon his settlement

among us. He built up our commerce, gave comfort to the doubting and timid, encouraged the emigration of industrious mechanics and tradesmen, founded the business of ship building, and directed the course of trade. His successful ventures for many years gave him the means of expending his wealth in decorating and improving the town. The memory of such a man is entitled to preservation and respect. He was literally, as well as figuratively, the *first merchant of Philadelphia* —the predecessor in whose footsteps have since walked hundreds of eminent mercantile characters, whose tact, ability, integrity and enterprise have made Philadelphia a magnificent city.

The following extracts from an article entitled "SAMUEL CARPENTER," in the *West Jersey Press*, by Hon. JOHN CLEMENT, Judge of New Jersey Court of Errors, will be found interesting:

* * * * * The social and religious intercourse that was constantly kept up between the settlements, introduced many business transactions, some of which involved the sale and purchase of real estate on one side of the stream to persons residing upon the opposite side; and it was frequently the case that persons in Pennsylvania owned considerable tracts of land in New Jersey, many of which were held for terms of years, and sometimes descending through several generations of the same family. Of these persons Samuel Carpenter was one; and identified him with the interests and advancement of the Province of West New Jersey,— although a non-resident,—the same as such as lived upon the soil, framed the government and administered the laws. The first purchase of land in New Jersey by Samuel Carpenter, was of Samuel Jennings in 1684, of six hundred acres, lying on the south side of Timber Creek, and with considerable front on the river Delaware. This included what has since become the valuable fisheries at Howell's Cove, but which at the time of purchase had no worth in the eyes of the contracting parties. These lands remained in the family for many years, passing to the son Samuel whose widow, Hannah, sold part thereof as executrix of her husband to Samuel Ladd, and through whom they descended to his daughter Deborah West.

In 1689 Samuel Carpenter bought fifty acres of William Roydon, situate in Newton Township, with a front on the river, which was part of the survey Roydon had previously made, extending from the river easterly to Cooper's Creek. Upon this now stands the principal part of the city of Camden, and which after several conveyances, became the property of William Cooper. The fifty acres extended along down the edge of the stream from near Market street, and back from the

shore, sufficiently far no doubt to get the full quantity, as called for in the deed. This however he sold the same year, and did not make any subsequent purchase of land in the township.

Next to William Penn he was considered the most wealthy person in the Province, for besides large mills at Bristol, Darby and Chester, and dwelling houses, warehouses, and wharves in Philadelphia, he also held nearly twenty thousand acres of land in different parts of the Province, and was largely engaged as a merchant. In 1693 he became a member of the Assembly, and a few years later, one of the Council, and ultimately Treasurer of the Province.

He took an active part in the political affairs of the City of Philadelphia, being for several years previous to 1712, one of the members of Council, and in 1701 also sat as a member of the Assembly, representing the largest constituency of any other person elected, and no doubt discharging many of the most important duties. Beside the real estate he held within the city bounds, he was also the owner of large tracts of land in the interior of the State, the grant for which was made directly to him from the Patroon. Near the mouth of the Schuylkill he had considerable marsh, which he improved into meadow, and which for many years was called Carpenter's Island.

*　　*　　*　　*　　*　　*　　*　　*　　*　　*　　*　　*

That Samuel Carpenter was a consistent and active member of the Society of Friends cannot be questioned. In Barbadoes there were many of this religious persuasion, and to which place nearly all who were ministers of that society, that visited America resorted before their return to England. This was before the settlements were attempted in Pennsylvania or New Jersey, and was looked upon as a place of banishment, for such as fell under the displeasure of the government, and whose adherence to their creed, and practice could not be abated by any of the punishments inflicted at home. A few years corrected much of the misery and destitution, that was intended by those in power, who not only imprisoned such as became subject to their tyranny, but robbed them of their property, and transported them without any means of future support, for in a short time those who had been previously sent for like offences, had by thrift and economy, secured enough to assist those who came under like circumstances, and render their condition comparatively comfortable.

Under the industry and perseverance of this class of citizens, the agricultural advantages of the Island were soon developed, and the increase of revenue to the

home Government, as well as large exportations made of the products, and sent to England for trade, appeared as a reproach upon those who had so shamelessly driven these people from their homes and estates, for opinion's sake.

The purchase of New Jersey and Pennsylvania by Friends, and whose enlarged and liberal form of government, was so attractive, opened an asylum for such as remained under persecution, to which they soon directed their footsteps, and laid the foundation for the institutions that now surround us, and where "none should make them afraid."

* * * * * * * * * * * * * *

That the subject of this sketch was always a resident of Philadelphia, and came to Philadelphia before the town had even assumed a shape, has generally been accepted as historical truth. Yet there is some doubt upon this point, as will appear from the following references : In Leaming and Spicer's revision of the laws of New Jersey, which also contains full lists of the members of the Legislature, may be found the name of Samuel Carpenter, as returned to represent the Third Tenth. This was in May 1685, and the inference would naturally follow that he resided within the limits of that division of the Province at that time, and was selected to look after the interests of the people in these parts. A note however, appended to the list says, "Robert Turner and Samuel Carpenter, appear not." Which shows that he did not participate in the proceedings at that time.

A curious feature of this session was that the Legislature sat but a single day, and in the words of the Resolve " agree to continue things upon the same foot and bottom, as formerly, until things shall be controverted in England, or the King's pleasure be further known therein." The day was spent in appointing Justices, Commissioners, Treasurers, Clerks, Sheriffs and Constables for the several divisions, and in assessing a general tax upon the people.

On the 25th of the ninth month in the same year, this body again assembled, at which time Samuel Carpenter appeared and took his seat, representing the Salem Tenth, and appointed one of the council. The sitting at that occasion was for nine days, in which time a number of salutary and useful laws were passed, and several resolutions acted upon, concerning the duties upon them.

JOSHUA, brother of SAMUEL CARPENTER, built *Grame Hall*, where in 1856, stood the Philadelphia Arcade. He was one of Penn's Commissioners for the sale of property, and in 1708 represented the city of Philadelphia in the Provincial Assembly. He was also one of the first Aldermen appointed under the charter of 1701. His burial place was the centre of what is now known as Washington Square. Joshua was an Episcopalian; he is said to have removed to Lancaster county, Pennsylvania. Some of his descendants settled in Western Pennsylvania, and others in Kent county, Delaware.

Children of Samuel and Hannah Carpenter:

I. HANNAH,
II. SAMUEL,
III. JOSHUA,
IV. JOHN,
V. REBECCA,
VI. ABRAHAM.

I. **Hannah,** born 1686, married WILLIAM FISHBOURNE, 1701, and died 1742. Her husband was Mayor of Philadelphia 1719–1720.

II. **Samuel,** (2d.) born in Philadelphia, February 9, 1788, married HANNAH, daughter of SAMUEL PRESTON, (and grand-daughter of THOMAS LLOYD,) 1711. She was born 1693, and died 1772.

III. **Joshua,** died in infancy.

IV. **John,** born 1690, married ANN HOSKINS, 1711, and died 1724. His wife died 1719. (The descent of this branch is given elsewhere.)

V. **Rebecca,** born 1692, died 1713.

VI. **Abraham,** died 1702.

Descent from Samuel Carpenter, Jr.:

Samuel Carpenter, (Jr.,) was a merchant of Philadelphia. and employed in the affairs of Provincial government. He married HANNAH PRESTON, 1711, and left five children, viz: SAMUEL, RACHEL, PRESTON, HANNAH and THOMAS.

I. **Samuel,** (3d.) died in Jamaica, 1747, leaving three children, SAMUEL, HANNAH, and THOMAS. He was a merchant, residing in Kingston. His two sons were educated in Edinburgh, and died in Kingston. Thomas left nine children—four boys and five girls.

II. **Rachel,** born 1716, died 1794, unmarried.

III. **Preston,** born 1721, and died October 20th, 1785. He married (1742) HANNAH, daughter of Samuel Smith, of Salem county, N. J. She was born 1723. He married secondly, Hannah Mason, but left no heirs.

IV. **Hannah,** married Samuel Shoemaker, 1746, and died 1766.

V. **Thomas,** died 1770, unmarried.

Descent from Preston and Hannah Carpenter:

I. HANNAH,
  II. SAMUEL PRESTON,
    III. ELIZABETH,
      IV. RACHEL,*
        V. MARY.
          VI. THOMAS,
            VII. WILLIAM,
              VIII. MARGARET,
                IX. JOHN,*
                  X. MARTHA.

Hannah Carpenter, daughter of PRESTON and HANNAH CARPENTER, born 1743, and died 1820, married CHARLES ELLET,† of New Jersey, 1768. Their children were

I. JOHN,
  II. SARAH,
    III. CHARLES,
      IV. WILLIAM,
        V. RACHEL CARPENTER,
          VI. MARY.

HANNAH ELLET, married secondly, JEDEDIAH ALLEN, whose daughter HANNAH, married JAMES SMITH, of Salem, New Jersey. Heirs—SARAH ANN, wife of Dr. David M. Davis, of Woodstown, New Jersey., who has heirs, and MARY, unmarried.

*Died young.

†CHARLES ELLET, had a daughter ELIZABETH, by a former wife—Sarah Austin. Elizabeth married Barzillia Lippincott, and removed to Alton, Ill. Their son, Gen. CHARLES LIPPINCOTT, distinguished himself in the Union army, during the war of the Rebellion. He recently occupied an important position in the House of Representatives at Washington, and is the present State Auditor of Illinois.

1. JOHN, eldest son of CHARLES and HANNAH ELLET, born 1769, and died May 10, 1824. He possessed an ample estate, and for the most of his life resided in Salem county, New Jersey. He married in 1792, MARY SMITH, of the same county. Her descent is as follows:

"In the ship "Charles and Edward," came from London, JOHN SMITH, SUSANNAH, his wife, two children, and servant,—landing at Salem, New Jersey, 4th mo. 1685." It is a matter of tradition that Susannah Smith was the daughter of a sea captain. On his return from a voyage, about the year 1662, he found the kingdom ravaged by the great plague, and his family, with this exception among the victims. Placing his daughter under guardianship, and providing for her education, he sailed upon a voyage from whence he never returned. The daughter married JOHN SMITH, and accompanied him to America. Her husband was a member of the Society of Friends, to which persuasion she became attached. He died 1723, occupying at the time a plantation called "Hedgefield," in the township of Mannington, Salem county, containing 1160 acres. The deed recites the grant by Charles II, to the Duke of York, of the Province of Nova Cesaria; from him to John Fenwick, of the estate in question; thence to Samuel Hedge, and from him to John Smith. His will is dated October 23, 1722, and bequeaths the plantation to his sons, JOHN, JOSEPH and WILLIAM, and daughter ELIZABETH. The descent is from JOHN SMITH, [2d,] whose son JOSEPH, married SARAH BASSETT; their son WILLIAM, married SARAH CHARLES, and their daughter MARY, (sister of the present JAMES SMITH, of Salem,) married JOHN ELLET.

Children of John and Mary Ellet:

I. HANNAH CARPENTER ELLET,
II. MARIA CHAMLES ELLET.

JOHN ELLET, married secondly, SARAH ENGLISH. Their children—

1. HENRY T. ELLET, ex-member of Congress from Mississippi, and a distinguished jurist of that State. He married REBECCA, daughter of ELIAS P SEELEY, ex-Governor of New Jersey. Their children are—JANE, JOSEPH, KATE, HENRY, and JOHN; 2, SARAH ENGLISH ELLET; 3, JOHN; 4. JOSEPH R.

HANNAH CARPENTER ELLET, daughter of JOHN and MARY ELLET, was born Nov. 22, 1793, and died April 20, 1862. She married GEORGE WISHART SMITH, of Virginia, 1813. At the time of his marriage he was a resident of Talbot County, Maryland, but subsequently removed to Philadelphia, where he died in 1821. The family have always claimed descent from the early settlers of the state, and without reference to the data in their possession, there seems conclusive evidence afforded by official records to identify them as early as 1700, when they occupied judicial and other responsible positions. From various circumstances—locality, alliance, and general surroundings—it is quite probable that they participated in the organization of the original Virginia Company, and were kinsmen of Sir Thomas Smith,* its President and chief manager. Under the primogeniture laws the estate descended to

---

*SIR THOMAS SMITH was successively Governor of the East India Company, Ambassador to Russia, King's Commissioner of the Navy, and President and Treasurer of the Virginia Company. How many of his kinsmen settled in America, is not known; but Capt. John Smith in his celebrated narrative, refers to Sir John, Sir William, and Sir Richard Smith, as having engaged in the adventure.

the eldest son, TULLY, who removed to and died in North Carolina; while GEORGE WISHART, THOMAS PERRIN, and CHARLES, with their sister ANN, took up their residence in Maryland. Thus the records, with slight exception, were conveyed to a distant state, and to which the compiler has not had reference. The testimony, from every quarter, concurs in representing the family as among the most respectable in their section. They intermarried with the Calverts, Singletons, Dudleys, Moseleys, Lauds, Scantlings, Keelings, and Hancocks, and are allied to families at present represented by some of the most prominent men of the State.

GEORGE WISHART SMITH was the son of PERRIN SMITH and MARGARET WISHART, his wife. The Wisharts were also early in the Colony—one of them a Member of the Virginia Parliament—"the first free Parliament ever held in America." One of Margaret Wishart's brothers, (Thomas,) lost his life in the Army of the Revolution, and another, (George,) was taken prisoner, and died at St. Augustine, Florida. PERRIN SMITH was the son of CHARLES SMITH and MARGARET PERRIN. (His estate was despoiled, and slaves carried off by the British and Refugees.) GEORGE WISHART SMITH served his country in the last war with Great Britain, as an officer in the "Maryland Line."

HANNAH CARPENTER SMITH, married, secondly, JOSEPH E. BROWN, of Salem, N. J. He died 1844, leaving WILLIAM HENRY, [who has heirs,] and JOSEPH FRANCIS. The latter served as Quarter Master, 12th Regt. N. J. Volunteers, of the Army of the Union, and died 1865, soon after the close of the war. WILLIAM HENRY also served in the same army.

Children of George W. and Hannah Carpenter Smith:

1. MARY ELLET SMITH, born in Talbot County, Maryland. Married Gen. RICHARD THOMAS, of Queen's Ann County, Maryland,—son of Capt. RICHARD THOMAS, U. S. Navy, (known in his day as "Truxton's fighting Lieutenant," in his fierce battles with the French and Algerines.) Their children—ANNA FRANCES and RICHARD. (The latter died young.)

2. MARGARET WISHART SMITH, died young.

3. CHARLES PERRIN SMITH, born in Philadelphia, removed to Salem, New Jersey, at an early age; has resided in Trenton since 1857; married HESTER A., daughter of Col. MATTHEW DRIVER, of Caroline County, Maryland. On her maternal side she is descended from Capt. PHILIP ALFORD, of the British Army, who came to Philadelphia from Barbadoes in 1684. CHARLES PERRIN SMITH, for a considerable period of his life was connected with the Editorial profession; served three years as State Senator; was appointed by Gov. William A. Newell, in 1857, Clerk of New Jersey Supreme Court; re-appointed by Gov. Charles S. Olden in 1862; and, a third time, re-appointed by Gov. Marcus L. Ward in 1867—upon the unanimous recommendation of the Judiciary, Bar and Union Press of the State—for terms of five years each. He was Chairman of the Union State Executive Committee during the war for the Union, and with the exception of a single year, has acted in that capacity to the present time.

Their children—

ELLEN WISHART, died 1858, aged 12 years.

CHARLES PERRIN, died 1864, aged 16.

ELIZABETH ALFORD SMITH.

FLORENCE BURMAN SMITH.

4. GEORGIANA WISHART SMITH, daughter of GEORGE W, and HANNAH CARPENTER SMITH married Col. SAMUEL C. HARBERT, of Philadelphia, (He served first as Quarter Master, and secondly as Paymaster, in the Union Army, during the entire war for the Union.) Their children are MARY VIRGINIA, and ELLA MARIA, WILLIAM ELLET, and several died young.

2. SARAH ELLET, daughter of CHARLES and HANNAH ELLET, born 1770, died 1824: married JOSEPH REEVES, of Salem county, N. J. Left no heirs.

3. CHARLES ELLET, son of CHARLES and HANNAH ELLET, born 1777, died 1847; married (1801,) MARY, daughter of ISRAEL ISRAEL, Esq., of Philadelphia. Mr. Israel, was a prominent and highly esteemed citizen,—a patriot, foremost in all good works. Among other positions, he occupied that of Sheriff of Philadelphia county; to which he was elected almost by acclamation. At the present time, (1870,) MARY ELLET survives, at the ripe age of ninety-one years. The following extract from a recent article by Colonel John W. Forney, published in the Philadelphia *Press*, truthfully and eloquently depicts her character:

"Her familiarity with American history for seventy-five years, including many of the characters who figured in and after the Revolution,—her patriotic ancestors and descendants,—her own passionate love of country, inherited from one and transmitted to the other,—her spotless reputation—entitle her, I think, more than any other of her sex, to the appellation of the "American Cornelia." In writing of her, I cherish no purpose of vain eulogy. I write solely to preserve the record of a remarkable life, that it may not be lost among men, and to present an example which every American woman may study with pleasure and with profit. * * * Rarely has there been such a resemblance between two persons, as between the illustrious Roman matron and MARY ELLET. Both renowned for purity of character, vigorous intellect, and a virtuous ambition, their love of country was supreme."

Heirs of Charles and Mary Ellet:

HANNAH, married George C. Hale, and left daughter Mary Anna, who married C. M. Crandell.

CHARLES,* (civil engineer,) married Elvira A., daughter of Judge William Daniels, of Lynchburgh, Virginia. They left four children,—Charles Rivers, Mary V., (married William Cabell, of Virginia,) Cornelia D., and William D. CHARLES RIVERS entered the service of his country as a Medical Cadet, under his father; was subsequently appointed Colonel, and served with distinction during the period of greatest trial on the Mississippi river.

*CHARLES ELLET, Jr., son of Charles and Mary Ellet, was born at Penn's Manor, Bucks county, Pennsylvania, 1810. He completed his education as civil engineer, in Paris, and upon returning to America, was appointed Assistant Engineer of the James river and Kanawha canal, then in course of construction, and of which he soon became chief. He was a thorough master of his profession, and his name became identified with many of the most important works in the country. Among those which he suggested and advocated at this period, may be mentioned the Wire Suspension Bridge across the Potomac at Georgetown, and another over the Mississippi at St. Louis. He constructed the temporary track of the Virginia Central railroad across the Blue Ridge, and contributed largely to the improvement of the Kanawha river. He also aided in laying out the Baltimore and Ohio railroad; and there are few, if any, of the Middle or Western States which do not furnish lasting evidence of his professional skill. Having twice had occasion to visit Europe, he was everywhere received and honored by the most prominent men of his profession. He published a volume entitled "The laws of trade in reference to works of internal improvement,"—an exhaustive treatise on the economy of traffic by canal, railroad and river; a paper on the physical geography of the Mississippi valley, pamphlets on coast and harbor defences, and other scientific works. In 1841 he planned and superintended the construction of the beautiful Wire Suspension Bridge across the Schuylkill, at Fairmount, Philadelphia,—the first of the kind on this continent. He served for several years as President of the Schuylkill Navigation Company. In 1847, he designed and constructed the first Suspension

bridge across Niagara river, near the cataract, and subsequently, the great Suspension bridge over the Ohio at Wheeling. He was appointed by the War Department to survey the lower Mississippi; and his report to the Government furnishes the most exact knowledge of the river and its confluent streams ever published. In 1853, appeared his two great works on the hydrography of the Ohio and Mississippi rivers, in which he disclosed a well matured plan for keeping the Ohio navigable at all seasons, by means of dykes and reservoirs; and another for deepening the mouths of the Mississippi. A distinguished writer in refering to this project says: "When we consider that the area drained by the Mississippi is a quarter of a million of miles square, and that ten thousand miles of its streams are navigable, we may gain some idea of the bold and magnificent scheme by which he proposed to maintain the navigation of the great rivers through the droughts of summer, by supplies to their volume of water from artificial lakes or reservoirs to be constructed on tributary streams."

While in Switzerland, he communicated to the Russian Government a detailed plan for converting war vessels into rams, by means of which they might raise the blockade of Sebastopol. The suggestions were cordially received, but owing to the death of the Emperor, and other causes having no reference to the merits of the project, not acted upon. He then earnestly addressed himself to his own Government, but the subject was dismissed with the reply that the Navy Department had no power, except by act of Congress, to experiment in the construction of vessels and machinery. At the outbreak of the rebellion Mr. Ellet repeatedly urged the importance of this matter upon the Navy Department, the President, and members of Congress, but without avail. At this time while there was a splendid army of two hundred thousand men within the defences of Washington, the enemy not only blockaded the Potomac, but carried off with impunity, locomotives and cars from under his guns. Undaunted by his frequent rebuffs, and sharing the general mortification at the untoward state of affairs, Mr. Ellet again came forward with practical recommendations. Having surveyed nearly every mile of the theatre of the war on the Potomac, and, as chief engineer of the Virginia Central Railway, perfectly familiar with the rolling-stock and transportation of the enemy, he felt competent to submit a plan for cutting the line of communication, and compelling them to retire from their aggressive position; and when it became apparent that a topographical map of Virginia could not be obtained, he offered the Government the benefit of what should have been regarded as invaluable experience. All his patriotic offers having been repelled by those who could not or would not comprehend the necessities of the hour, he felt

impelled from a sense of duty, to appeal to Congress and the nation. His pamphlets attracted general attention, and stamped their author as a man conversant with the scientific principles of warfare. In his famous letter to the President, October 1861, he wrote :

"You are aware, Sir, that I have for many weeks been endeavoring to obtain an interview with the Major-General, for the purpose of submitting to him the evidence that the rebel army, which has so long threatened this capital is wholly dependent for its existence as an organized body, on the Orange and Alexandria railroad, and the extensions of that work to Richmond, and to the west and southwest ; that the destruction of that road and its motive power, as matters now stand, would be equivalent to the destruction and disastrous dispersion of the army which it supplies with food, munitions of war, and reinforcements ; this road and all its connections north of James river, are very deficient of locomotive engines and rolling stock ; vital facts, on which I have a right to ask to be heard, because as an engineer long in the actual professional control of large portions of these works, I was necessarily very familiar with their condition.

Based upon these facts, I desired to submit to the commanding general, a plan by which this already exceedingly deficient supply of locomotive engines could be almost instantaneously reduced ; the railroad line which sustains the rebel army, and all its tributaries, could be for a season disabled ; and how a strong division might then be placed between that army, thus crippled, and its sources of supply, both to prevent it from restoring its communications, and to cut off its inevitable retreat.

The plan, in fact, contemplated the immediate and entire destruction of the insurgent army without bloodshed ; provided only that the facts could be submitted to the general in command, and he would have the prudence to act upon them with absolute secrecy and prompt dispatch.

*   *   *   *   *   *   *   *   *   *   *   *

Let me repeat the statement of a transparent fact. The true base of the rebel army of the Potomac, is Manassas Junction. From that point all supplies are now conveyed to the army north of the Junction by common teams. But south of this true base—unlike the great armies of past times—they have no common road transportation, but depend wholly on their railroads. These railroads and the country which they traverse, from Manassas Junction to the Gulf of Mexico, are, in a military sense, wholly unprotected. Even now you may strike in south of that position—almost anywhere with a small division under a gallant leader, and make southwardly almost with impunity ; disabling the rail ways and machinery as you advance, to prevent pursuit by the rebel army of the Potomac, and avoiding the large cities if you have not force sufficient to take them. It will be unnecessary to invest these cities even to render them harmless. By temporarily crippling their railroads and canals merely, they will be sufficiently invested.

By disabling the unprotected railroads and machinery south of Manassas, you will at once place the rebel army before Washington, starving and helpless, at the mercy of your general here,—provided, he is then able to put any part of his vast, patriotic and fiery masses in forward motion."

"Victories upon victories in Kentucky, and on the Mississippi, though purchased by torrents of the dearest blood of the West, will leave the rebellion in full vigor, in a more contracted field perhaps ; though even that is doubtful, but more concentrated, and in undiminished strength. The rebellion must be essentially crushed, if at all, quickly ; and it must receive its death-blow in Virginia, where the military strength of its upholders is chiefly concentrated. It must be broken down by the capture, or by the irretrievable defeat of the rebel army at Manassas."

The same writer referred to, says: "What a commentary is this upon the strategy of those unhappy times? Experience proved that Mr. Ellet was right. The rebel army was finally crippled and destroyed, by the destruction of its communications." Read in the light of subsequent events, the pamphlets seem almost prophetic.

When the effectiveness of the ram was demonstrated at Hampton Roads by the loss of two of our frigates; and the great peril of all of our sea-board cities only averted by what seemed the merest accident, Mr. Ellet's renewed and persistent representations finally received attention, and he was engaged by the Secretary of War, under a contract, to construct and test wooden rams on the Western rivers. The best he could do under the circumstances, was to secure a number of tugs and side-wheel steamers, strengthen their bows with solid timber, protect their boilers with double tiers of oak, and plate the pilot houses against musketry. *These rams were not to be accepted until their efficacy should be proved in battle;* for which an opportunity soon offered. The Navy regarded the project with marked disfavor, and the river craftsmen saw all kinds of obstacles in the way. Great difficulty was also experienced in procuring engineers, pilots and crews.

His brother ALFRED W. ELLET, then a captain in the Fifty-ninth Illinois, brought his own company, with another from the Thirty-third Illinois, and joined the rams at Cairo. The enemy had thirteen gunboats, eight of which could be used as rams. They attacked the National fleet on the 10th of May, 1862, and sunk the Cincinnati and Mound City. About this time ALFRED W. ELLET, was sent down with five boats, and such crews as he could collect. He was soon joined by Col. CHARLES ELLET, with several side-wheel boats, who begged Com. Davis for permission to engage the hostile fleet below. The rams had not a gun on board larger than a musket, but were each provided with twenty sharp-shooters, who fired from loop-holes. During the night of the 11th, Alfred floated down in a yawl, to a point opposite the fort, and discovering that it had been evacuated, at daylight raised his flag on the works. At 4½ A. M., the rams had steamed down the river, and reached the gunboats drawn out in front of the city. The enemy were concealed by a bend in the river below. Col. Ellet had received no notification from the Commodore that an engagement was imminent, and was first warned by the guns of the enemy. He at once crowded steam, and standing upon the deck of the Queen of the West, shouted to his brother on the Monarch, "Follow me and attack the enemy." Eighty, ninety, one hundred pounds of steam were successively reported. Dashing outside of the line of gunboats, so as to get a clear view of the enemy, and a fair sweep against them, he shot past Com. Davis' fleet, and plunged

against the ram and gunboat, Gen. Lovel. The crash was tremendous. The
Queen's chimneys reeled and shook, the upper works of both boats were shattered,
and for a moment it seemed as if they would both go down together. In five
minutes the Lovell had sunk. The Queen was immediately attacked by the Bragg
and Price. The former struck the Queen disabling one of her wheels; glancing
off, she struck her rebel consort, the Price, and sinking her. At this instant down
came the Monarch, and rushed into the Beauregard. Col. Charles Ellet, in his
report, said: "The Monarch passed ahead of our gunboats, and went most
gallantly into action. She first struck the rebel boat that struck my flag ship, and
sunk her. She was then struck by one of the enemy's rams, but not injured. She
then pushed on and struck the Beauregard, and burst open her side. The Monarch
then pushed at the gunboat Little Rebel, the flag-ship, and having slight headway,
pushed her before her,—the commander and crew escaping. The Monarch finding
the Beauregard sinking, took her in tow, and she sank in shoal water. She then
dashed after the two or three retreating vessels, but their start enabled them to
escape." The Jeff. Thompson ran upon the Arkansas shore, where she was blown
up. All who were not wounded, escaped to the woods, persued by exploding
shells. The Sumpter was abandoned. The Little Rebel, crippled by shot and
pursued by a ram, plunged upon the shore and her crew escaped. In their consternation, three of the enemy's rams ran into each other, and while thus entangled, the
gunboats riddled their hulls and upper works. The Van Dorn fled, pursued by
the Monarch and Lancaster. Never was victory more prompt or decisive. In an
hour every vessel of the enemy's fleet but one, was sunk, burnt, blown up or
captured. While the battle was in progress, the bluffs at Memphis were lined with
spectators. Col. Ellet sent his son, Charles Rivers, and nephew, Edward, with a
small party, to demand the surrender of the city. Having delivered the message,
the two young men proceeded to the Post Office, followed by an infuriated mob,
and raised the Union flag upon that building. Col. Ellet was disabled by a shot in
the knee, and the command devolved upon his brother Alfred. He was conveyed
to Cairo, on the Switzerland, where he expired, on the 21st of June. His remains
were taken to Philadelphia, received by the municipal authorities, and deposited
in Independence Hall, from whence he was interred at Laurel Hill Cemetery
with distinguished civic and military honors. His wife survived him but a few
days. Her death was the result of grief and over exhaustion.

Col. Alfred Ellet, now in command of the ram fleet, without a single piece of
artillery on board, and unaccompanied by the national gunboats, started with the
rams alone, to co-operate with Admiral Farragut, then known to be ascending the

river. Having reached a point a short distance above Vicksburgh, and deeming it important to communicate with the national fleet below the batteries, despatches were prepared, and CHARLES RIVERS and EDWARD, (Col. Ellet's stripling son,) were sent overland to convey them to the Admiral. Making their way through the deep and stagnant swamps on the western bank of the Mississippi, at times eluding the enemy's pickets by concealing themselves in the tangled underwood, or rushing into the water, they spent the night in crossing the isthmus, and next morning covered with mud, emerged from the fog and swamp on the river bank opposite the fleet. They were taken on board the Hartford, and after examination, sent back with despatches, under a large escort

In the meantime, Col. ALFRED W. ELLET, had steamed up the Yazoo, on the Monarch, and was soon followed by CHARLES R. ELLET, on the Lancaster, to Liverpool Landing, where they compelled the enemy to burn three of their gunboats, the Van Dorn, Livingston and Lady Polk, to avoid capture. The siege of Vicksburgh followed, with various expeditions up the different rivers. Then came the enemy's plated ram Arkansas, severely handling two of the national vessels, daringly running through the fleet, and taking refuge under the Vicksburgh batteries. The consternation occasioned by her apparent invulnerbility, was indescribable. There was fear that she might return and sink the entire thirty vessels. In this emergency, Col. ALFRED W. ELLET, *volunteered to go down on the Queen of the West, and destroy the Arkansas under the batteries.* He started on the 22d of July, the Essex at first leading, and followed by the Benton. Soon the Queen of the West rushed past the other steamers, to plunge at full speed into the Arkansas. She ran into the landing through a tempest of fire, that rained missiles upon every part of her, with the design of breaking the Arkansas to pieces, by a butt just forward her side-guns, but this was prevented by her swinging in the stream as the ram approached. The stroke was thus made a glancing one. The concussion, however, was heavy, and a number of the Arkansas crew sprang overboard, under the impression that she was sinking. The Queen then backed out, and ran in again to give the enemy another butt, but missed her, and struck the shore, straining her bow timbers, and creating apprehensions for her own safety. As the Queen ran into the stream, the guns on the bluff opened with redoubled fury, pouring upon the exposed ram a storm of iron, to which she made no reply. Round shot and shell of all sizes, and grapeshot passed through the chimneys and struck the boat at almost every point. Both escape pipes were cut off a few feet above the deck; round shot passed through the bales of hay erected as a barricade in front of the boilers; a sixty-four pound shot struck the stern, and passed in a straight line

the entire length of the boat, going through the state-room, bulk heads, and smashed to atoms an iron safe; the braces were shot away; one shot lodged in the engine room, and shells burst in various parts of the boat. The daring ram thus terribly battered, succeeded in making her way back to the fleet above.

In August the first siege of Vicksburgh was abandoned; the lower fleet passed down to New Orleans, and the gun boats returned to Helena. About this period the Benton, with the Rams Monarch, Lancaster, and others, captured the steamer Fair Play, with a cargo of five thousand muskets, and a large amount of ammunition, equipments, &c.

On the first of November the Marine Brigade was ordered to be raised for the purpose of keeping the river open. On the 5th, Charles Rivers Ellet was commissioned as Colonel, and placed in command of the Ram Fleet, while his uncle Alfred, as Brigadier General, took command of the Marine Brigade. This was an independent command, composed of cavalry, artillery and riflemen, conveyed on seven large bullet proof steamers, fitted for the accommodation of cavalry. Wherever guerillas infested the banks, or the enemy discovered throwing up batteries, these steamers were run along-side the shore, gang-planks conveniently arranged, swung out, and in the course of a few moments mounted troops scoured the adjacent country and captured or destroyed the fugitives. In one of the many conflicts Gen. Ellet's horse was shot under him, and he had other narrow escapes. By the energetic operations of this brigade the river was not only kept open, but the enemy cut off from his supplies in Arkansas and Texas.

On the 29th December, Gen. Sherman and Admiral Porter determined to force the passage of the Yazoo. Haines' Bluff was covered with batteries, and the river obstructed by large rafts of timber. Col. Charles Rivers Ellet *volunteered to lead the way to the batteries, and blow up the raft.* A torpedo was fitted to the ram Lioness, and Col. Ellet waited on Admiral Porter to say that he had two tons of powder at the bow of his boat, and asked for instructions. He was directed to steam directly up to the raft, which was within fifty feet of the heavy batteries, and blow it up. Admiral Porter thus refers to the undertaking:

"Ten thousand men were to have been thrown right at the foot of the cliffs, risking the loss of the transports, while all the iron-clads were to open fire on the batteries and try and silence them temporarily. The ram Lioness under Colonel Ellet, was fitted with an apparatus for breaking torpedo wires, and was to go ahead and clear the way. Colonel Ellet was also provided with fifteen torpedoes to blow up the raft, and enable the vessels to get by if possible. *This desperate duty he took upon himself cheerfully, and no doubt would have performed it well had the opportunity occurred.* The details of the expedition were left to me, and it was all ready to start at 3.30 A. M. A dense fog unfortunately set in at midnight and lasted until morning, when

it was too late to start. It was so thick that vessels could not move. Men could not see each other at ten paces. The river is too narrow for operations in clear weather, much less in a fog. After the fog, there was in the afternoon every indication of a long and heavy rain."

In the spring of 1863 the enemy brought out a large steamer, the City of Vicksburgh, armed and fully prepared for desperate service: and on the 2d of February, Admiral Porter ordered Col. Charles Rivers Ellet to destroy her at Vicksburgh Landing. The next morning he ran the Queen of the West, under the batteries, while exposed to a terrific fire, and aimed to strike the iron-clad amid-ships, but she was moored in such a position that it was found impossible to give full effect to the blow. At the moment of contact, the Queen discharged three incendiary projectiles into the cotton barricades, and set her on fire. At the same time the Queen also took fire, the flames spreading rapidly, and the dense smoke driving the engineers from their posts. Under the circumstances the blow could not be repeated, and pointing the steamer down stream, she ran the entire length of the batteries, under a storm of shot and shell. The flames were extinguished by throwing overboard the blazing cotton. Once below Vicksburgh, the Queen nearly swept the river of the enemy's transports and gunboats. In the course of three days she captured or destroyed three large steamers, loaded with stores valued at about a half million of dollars. She was finally captured while aground in Red River, within range of several formidable batteries, but the commander and most of the crew escaped on a prize steamer. On their way up the river they received not less than two hundred shots from different batteries. The Queen was soon afterwards destroyed by the enemy to prevent re-capture. Admiral Farragut subsequently ran the batteries at Port Hudson with the Hartford and Albatross, and ordered several of the rams to join him below Vicksburgh. The Switzerland, under the command of Charles R. Ellet, and the Lancaster, under command of Lieut-Col. John A. Ellet, cousin to the General, started to obey this order. In passing the batteries of Vicksburgh, for the space of about three miles, they were assailed by a shower of missiles of every description. The boilers of the Switzerland were pierced, and she was instantly enveloped in scalding steam; while the Lancaster riddled by heavy shot, soon became unmanageable, and in a sinking condition. The conduct of her commander, Lieut-Col. John A. Ellet, is described as heroic. Having seen his crew safely in the boats, he fired the cotton barricades, and after great peril succeeded in reaching his crippled consort, helplessly drifting down the current, until she reached the national fleet below, and was taken in tow by the Albatross. The Switzerland subsequently performed important patrol and dispatch duty between the armies of Gen. Grant and Gen. Banks. Charles Rivers Ellet, at this period, was but twenty years and five months of age. He was

remarkable for acuteness and activity of intellect, and read and discussed with
great avidity the most celebrated philosophical authors of the world. He died
suddenly at the residence of his uncle, Dr. Edward Ellet, Bunker Hill, Ill., on the
night of 16th October, 1863, and was interred at Laurel Hill Cemetery, Philadelphia.

[A portion of the foregoing account of the services of the Ram Fleet on the
Mississippi, is condensed from an able article by John S. C. Abbott, in *Harper's
Monthly Magazine.*]

Mary Ellet, married James Bailey.

John I. Ellet, married first, Laura Scarrett. Heirs—Col. John A. Ellet,
Charles, Richard, (Lieutenant of Cavalry, Mississippi Marine Brigade; married Bettie Cullen.)

John I. Ellet, married secondly, Mary Skillman, and by her had eight
children.

Col. John A. Ellet, (his son,) was appointed to command the Ram Fleet at the
time Brigadier Gen. A. W. Ellet, was detached to organize the Mississippi River
Marine Brigade, of which the Ram Fleet formed a part. He distinguished himself
on various occasions, and particularly at the time ot the loss of his Ram, the
' Lancaster," while passing the Vicksburgh batteries, to support Admiral Farragut.
(See art. on services of Ram Fleet.)

Richard, his brother, enlisted in a corps organized in California, was attached
to a Massachusetts regiment of cavalry, severely wounded in one of the many fights
on the Peninsula, promoted to a Lieutenancy in the Mississippi Marine Brigade,
and served with distinction during and after the struggle to open the Mississippi
river to the Gulf.

Eliza Ellet, married George S. Bryan; left daughter Mary E., who
married Robert Albree.

Edward C. Ellet, (M. D., near Alton, Illinois,) married Lydia Little, of
New Jersey. Surviving children, Annie and Lillie.

*Alfred W. Ellet married Sarah J. Robarts, of Philadelphia. Heirs—
Edward C., William H., and Elvira A.

*See art. on services of Ram Fleet.

Edward C. Ellet, Jr., enlisted at the commencement of the war, before he had reached his sixteenth year. He served under Gen. Prentice during the early campaigns in Eastern Missouri, was transferred to to his father's regiment, 9th Missouri vols., and served in the campaigns under Fremont and Curtis, in Southwestern Missouri, until after the victory at Pea Ridge; accompanied his father to the Ram Fleet participated in the great victory off Memphis, was appointed aid on his father's staff, and remained in the service until the Marine Brigade had performed its specific duties and was disbanded.

4. WILLIAM, son of CHARLES and HANNAH ELLET, born 1775, married Elizabeth Taggert, of New Jersey. He died in New York 1836, where for many years he had been a prominent citizen. He left three heirs— Sarah Ann, William H, and Charles.

WILLIAM H. ELLET was born in New York, and graduated in Columbia College. He studied medicine, and the Doctor's degree was conferred upon him by the Rutger's Medical Faculty of Geneva College, about the year 1828. In 1833 he was elected Professor of Experimental Chemistry in Columbia College. Three years afterwards he was chosen Professor of Chemistry and Physics in the College of South Carolina, in which capacity he taught with great success for thirteen years, and then returned to his native city, where he resided until his death in 1859. The Medical Faculty of Geneva College conferred upon him a gold medal for his learned dissertation on the compounds of Cyanogen, and the Legislature of South Carolina presented him with a valuable service of silver plate for the discovery of a new and cheap method of preparing gun-cotton, which, it was thought, would cause an increased demand for one of the staple products of that State. Dr. ELLET, for the remainder of his life, was consulting chemist of the Manhattan Gas Company. In every thing relating to the chemistry of gas manufacture, he is said to have had no superior in this country. He was a man of sound learning, extensive and varied attainments, and of highly cultivated taste. He married ELIZABETH F., daughter of Dr. William N. Lummis, a physician of some eminence in northern New York. Mrs. Ellet is a lady of excellent literary reputation, and her various works in prose and poetry enjoy well-deserved popularity.

CHARLES ELLET resided for some years in California, but returned to New York about the year 1859, where he engaged in business. He was assassinated in the summer of 1868.

5. RACHEL CARPENTER, daughter of CHARLES and HANNAH ELLET, born 1780, and died 1855; married JAMES WAINWRIGHT, Esq., of Maryland. She was an effective Minister of the Society of Friends. Their children—

1. WILLIAM J. WAINWRIGHT married Sarah Church of New Jersey. He was for many years a merchant, Member of Select Council, and, in other respects, a prominent and esteemed citizen of Philadelphia. He died 1869.

2. THOMAS B. WAINWRIGHT was a merchant in Pittsburgh, Pa. He married Emily Watson, and left RACHEL, CAROLINE, (who married Hiram Kimball,) JOHN WATSON, (Lieutenant of Cavalry in Union Army during the War of the Rebellion, under Buell and Rosecrans in the Western and South-Western campaigns;) ALICE and SALLIE E.

3. JAMES ELLET WAINWRIGHT married Mary Delaney, of Delaware, and left two heirs—Mary and Charles L.

JAMES ELLET was among the earlier adventurers to California; was the first County Clerk elected in San Francisco, and, for a number of years, one of the most prominent and influential citizens of the place. He subsequently resided in China and Japan, and lost his life by the sinking of the Japanese War Ram *Talla-hasse*, near Yokohama, in 1869.

6. MARY, daughter of Charles and Hannah Ellet, born 1782, and died. unmarried, 1821.

III. **Elizabeth Carpenter,** daughter of PRESTON and Hannah Carpenter, married EZRA FIRTH, of Salem County, N. J. Their children were—

1. PRESTON, who left three children—Maria West, Hannah Evans, and Lucas.

2. JOHN, married ANN, daughter of Thomas Thompson, of Salem, N. J. Their children—Hannah Reynolds, Thomas, John, and Samuel. Hannah Reynold's heirs are Benjamin, Edward and Thompson.

3. THOMAS, left three sons and one daughter.

4. SAMUEL, left two daughters, Mary and Sarah, both in South Carolina. Mary married Philip Givins, and has three daughters and a son.

5. HANNAH, married Isaac C. Jones. Their children: 1 Samuel T. (married first, Sarah Thomas, and, secondly, Martha Thomas;) 2. Aquilla, 3. Lydia, (married Dr. Caspar Wistar.) 4. Franklin, 5. Mary C. Williams; 6. Isaac C. (married Sarah W. Woodruff,) and 7. Hannah E. married Lloyd Pearsall Smith, of Philadelphia.

V. **Mary Carpenter,** daughter of Preston and Hannah Carpenter, married SAMUEL TONKINS. She was born 1750, and died 1821.

VI. **Thomas Carpenter,** son of Preston and Hannah Carpenter, born 1752, married Mary Tonkins, and left EDWARD, who was born 1772, and married Sarah, daughter of James Stratton, M. D., of Swedesborough, sister of Ex-Governor Charles C. Stratton. Edward Carpenter died 1813, and left

1. THOMAS P. CARPENTER, (Counsellor-at Law, and Ex-Justice New Jersey Supreme Court,) married Rebecca, daughter of Dr. Samuel Hopkins, of Philadelphia. Children—Susan Mary, Anna S., Thomas P. and James H. Carpenter.

2. MARY T. CARPENTER married Richard W. Howell, Counsellor of Supreme Court, New Jersey. Heirs, 1. Samuel B. (M. D., of Philadelphia.) 2. Charles S., 3. Joshua L., 4. Thomas J., [Lieut. 3d N. J. Vols., killed at battle of Gaines Mills, 1862,] 4. Anna, wife of Malcom Lloyd, 5. Francis L.

3. JAMES S. CARPENTER married Camilla Sanderson. Heirs, John T., Sarah S., Sophia C., Cornelia M., James E. and Preston.

4. SAMUEL T. CARPENTER married Frances Champlain, of Connecticut. Heirs—Samuel C. B. and Frances Mary.

5. EDWARD CARPENTER married Anna Maria Howe. Heirs—Lewis H., James E., Sarah C., Mary H., Casper W. and Thomas P.

VII. **William Carpenter**, son of Preston and Hannah Carpenter, born 1751, died 1837. Married first, ELIZABETH WYATT, [born 1764, died 1790.] Their children were: 1. MARY WYATT, born 1783, died 1836, [she married James Hunt, of Penna., and left two sons, John and William, and daughters Mary, Naomi and Hannah,] 2. HANNAH born 1785, died young.

WILLIAM CARPENTER married secondly, 1801, Mary Redman, born 1779, and died 1816. Their heirs

1. WILLIAM married first, Hannah Scull, and secondly, Phebe Warren.

2. JOHN REDMAN, unmarried. He was a young man of unusual talents, and at the time of his death [1833] Cashier of the Branch Bank of the United States at Buffalo, New York.

3. RACHEL R. married Charles Sheppard. Heirs—William C., [who married Hannah E. Zornes,] and John R. C.

4. HANNAH, died young.

5. SAMUEL PRESTON CARPENTER [present Surrogate of Salem County, N. J.,] married Hannah, daughter of Benjamin and Sarah W. Acton. Heirs— John Redman Carpenter [married Mary C., daughter of Joseph B. Thompson,] Sarah Wyatt [married Richard H. Reeves,] Samuel Preston, Jr., [married Rebecca Bassett,] William.

SAMUEL P. CARPENTER married secondly, Sarah Sheppard.

VIII. **Margaret Carpenter**, daughter of Preston and Hannah Carpenter, married JAMES M. WOODNUTT, of Salem County, N. J. Heirs— Hannah, Sarah, Thomas, Jonathan, Preston, Elizabeth, Margaret, William, Mary, and Martha. Of these

HANNAH married Clement Acton, of Salem, N. J. Heirs—1, Clement J. [married Mary, daughter of Col. John Noble. Their Children—Margaret W., William W., Eliza N., and Elizabeth.] 2, Margaret, married John Griscom, M. D., of Philadelphia. Heirs—Clement, [married Frances C. Biddle,] John D., Hannah W., and William W.

JONATHAN married Mary Goodwin. Heirs—Richard, married Lydia Hall—their children, Mary, Emily, Sarah, Margaret, and Richard H.; William, married Elizabeth Bassett—their children, Joseph, Jonathan, Thomas, Anna, Clement, Howard, and William; Thomas, married Hannah H. Morgan—children, Abbie M., William and Clement A.; Mary married Edward A. Acton, [who was killed in the Union Army during the war of the Rebellion]—children, Walter, Isaac O., and Jonathan.

JONATHAN married secondly, Sarah Dennis,

PRESTON married Rachel Goodwin. Heirs—Elizabeth, married Ansley Newlin, James M., married Elizabeth Denn, and has heirs; Edward died in California, unmarried; Preston C. and Hannah Ann, (who married Nathan Baker, and left Preston and Mary.)

MARGARET, married William J. Shinn.* Heirs—Emeline, Samuel, Mary [married Dr. Thomas Reed, of Philadelphia, and left heirs,] Martha, [married Dr. Isaiah D. Clawson, of Salem County, N. J.]

MARTHA WOODNUTT married Joshua Reeves of Salem County, and left heirs. She died in 1869.

MARY WOODNUTT married Benjamin Newlin, of Pennsylvania.

X. Martha Carpenter, daughter of Preston and Hannah Carpenter, married Joseph Reeves, of Salem County, N. J. Heirs—Samuel, Milicent, Joseph and Mary,

* WILLIAM J. SHINN was for many years one of the most useful and influential men of his section; serving the public in various capacities, but more prominently as Judge of Common Pleas, Member of the State Senate, and President of the Bank. He was the father-in-law of Hon. Isaiah D. Clawson, late Member of Congress, and uncle of Hon. William S. Clawson, Judge of New Jersey Supreme Court. Few men have been more highly esteemed for their genial disposition and genuine goodness of heart. He died in the 78th year of his age.

Descendants of John Carpenter,

(SECOND SON OF SAMUEL CARPENTER, SEN.)

John Carpenter married ANNE, daughter of Richard and Esther Hoskins, 11 mo., 11, 1710.

RICHARD HOSKINS, was "an eminent Physician and Minister of the Gospel." He died in England on a visit about 1700. His wife died in Philadelphia, in 1698. He left several daughters.

MARTHA CARPENTER, daughter of JOHN and ANNE, married in Philadelphia. REESE MEREDETH, 8 mo., 23, 1738. REESE was a son of REESE, of Radnorshire, Wales. He produced a certificate dated 2d mo., 1730, from the Monthly Meeting in Leominster, Hereford county, Great Britain, of his right of membership among Friends. Died in Philadelphia, November 17, 1778, aged about 70. His wife died 8 mo. 26, 1769. He was a shipping merchant, largely in trade. Their children were: SAMUEL, married MARGARET CADWALADER; ANNE, married HENRY HILL, merchant; ELIZABETH, married GEORGE CLYMER.

GEORGE CLYMER was born in Philadelphia, June 10, 1739. His grandfather, Richard Clymer, was a shipping merchant. His children were CHRISTOPHER and WILLIAM. CHRISTOPHER married DEBORAH, daughter of George Fitzwater, 1734. GEORGE CLYMER was their only child. George Fitzwater, was a shipping merchant, son of Thomas Fitzwater, "a Minister

*I am indebted to NATHAN KITE, late of Philadelphia, THOMAS WILLING CLYMER, of Trenton, and "FRIENDS' RECORDS," for the genealogy of this branch of the family.

among Friends," who married Elizabeth Palmer, 1684. His son. George,
married Mary, daughter of Abraham Hardiman, "a much esteemed member
of the Society of Friends," whose second wife was Rebecca, daughter of John
Willsford, of New Jersey, "a noted Minister of the Gospel among Friends."
ABRAHAM HARDIMAN died soon after his second marriage, 11 mo., 10, 1698.
He was brother of HANNAH CARPENTER, as appears by a letter of SAMUEL
CARPENTER, extant, in memoirs of WILLIAM and ALICE ELLIS. He was a
merchant. His children by first marriage were MARY, (married GEORGE
FITZWATER,) HANNAH married GILBERT FALCONER, and DEBORAH married
GEORGE CLAYPOOL. GILBERT FALCONER, was son of David Falconer, merchant, of Edinburgh, Scotland. The CARPENTERS sign the marriage certificates of the three daughters of Abraham Hardiman, as near relatives. The
nearest of kin who sign the marriage certificates of George and Mary Fitzwater, were Thomas Fitzwater, his brother, John Palmer, his half brother,
Samuel and Hannah Carpenter, Samuel and John, their sons, Hannah, their
daughter, and her husband William Fishbourne, Hannah Hardiman, the bride's
sister, Thomas Mitchell, Thomas Iredell and Rebecca his wife, Sarah Story,
Catharine Jones, and Susannah Woodworth. Thomas Mitchell married Sarah,
daughter of John and Sarah Denny. Samuel and Hannah Carpenter sign
their marriage certificate as "nearest relatives after the bride's mother."
Thomas Iredell came in 1703 from England to Philadelphia. His wife was
Rebecca Williams. They were married 3d mo., 9, 1705. The near relatives signing the marriage certificate, were Hannah Carpenter, her son John,
her daughter and son-in-law, Hannah and William Fishbourne, and the
three daughters of Abraham Hardiman, Mary, Hannah and Deborah.

The children of George Fitzwater and Mary Hardiman, his wife, were:—
Hannah married William Coleman; Deborah, married Christopher Clymer;
Elizabeth married James House: Martha married James Morris· Mary,
married Francis Richardson; Sarah, married Isaac Griffith; ———, married
——— Hogg.

WILLIAM COLLMAN was a son of William Coleman, merchant, intimate with Dr. Benjamin Franklin for forty years, and highly spoken of in Franklin's Autobiography. He married Hannah Fitzwater in 1737, died 1769, leaving no children, but brought up his nephew GEORGE CLYMER, and left him a large portion of his property. George Clymer signed the Declaration of Independence, was a member of the Federal Convention, and first Congress, and a prominent and honored patriot in the early days of the Republic.

The children of Martha and James Morris were George and Phœbe; of Mary and Francis Richardson, Mary, Grace and Hannah; of Sarah and Isaac Griffiths, Mary and Elizabeth; of Mrs. Hogg, Peregrine and Mary.

Francis Richardson, son of Francis R. and Mary, was a captain in the King's Life Guards, and his sister Mary married Clement Biddle. George Fitzwater died 1750, leaving a large estate.

GEORGE CLYMER lost both of his parents before he was a year old, and went to live with his uncle and aunt Coleman, June 1, 1740. He was a merchant, in partnership with his father and brother-in-law, Reese and Samuel Meredith. Elizabeth, eldest daughter of Reese and Martha Meredith, (whom he married in 1765,) was his fifth cousin through the Hardimans. He died in Morrisville, Pa., January 23, 1813, at the residence of his son, Henry Clymer, and was buried in Friends' ground, Trenton. His wife died in Northumberland, Pa., February 1815. Their children,—1, William Coleman, and 2, Julian, died young; 3, Henry; 4, Meredith, (died 1794 on Monongahela river, from exposure with the City Troop, during the "Whiskey Insurrection;") 5, Margaret, married George McCall; died in Philadelphia 1799; heirs, George Clymer and William Coleman McCall; (the latter was a Surgeon in the Navy, and married Mary, sister of Philemon Dickinson, Esq., of Trenton.) 6, Ann, married Charles Lewis, of England, in 1807, and died in Trenton, August 1810; 7, George married Maria O'Brien, of Philadelphia, and died July 28, 1848. His wife died in Trenton, September 1853, leaving son Meredith.

HENRY CLYMER married Mary, daughter of Thomas Willing, merchant in
Philadelphia, July 9, 1794; heirs—1, Eliza, married Edward Overton, counsellor, May 2, 1818; 2, Louisa and Ann died young; 3, William Bingham,
married Mary Hiester Clymer, (his fifth cousin,) of Reading, Pa., August 11,
1852, their children Mary, Richard W., Maria and Rosa N.; 4, Thomas Willing Clymer; 5, George Clymer, Surgeon U. S. N., married Mary, daughter of Admiral Shubrick, May 8, 1845, and resides in Washington, D. C.,
their children Mary W. and Shubrick, [three died young;] 6. Francis Clymer; 7, Mary Willing Clymer.   Thomas W. and Mary W. reside in Trenton, N. J.

Addenda.

Bishop Meade[*] in his work "THE OLD CHURCHES AND FAMILIES OF VIRGINIA," clearly indicates that the Virginia branch of the compilers family were among the first who arrived in the colony. He says: "Cape Henry, in Princess Anne County and Parish, was probably the first point at which our Virginia colonists touched on reaching America. Here a fort was established, either then or soon after. At what time other settlements were made on the coast and bay, cannot certainly be determined; but there is every reason to believe it must have been at a very early period. In the year 1642, we find the Parish recognized as existing. How long before this it had been a congregation, we cannot ascertain." The Bishop publishes extracts from the Church records, and the names of Mosely, Land, Singleton, Smith, Hancock and others, known to have been allied by marriage, are given from time to time as vestrymen. The Rev. Robert Dickson, who officiated at the marriage of Perrin Smith and Margaret Wishart, was Rector of this church for nearly twenty years, at a salary of sixteen thousand pounds of tobacco. The Rev. Cornelius Calvert, (husband of Dian, sister of Margaret Wishart,) was also a Rector of this Parish. As the soil became exhausted from the culture of tobacco, and other causes, many of the descendents removed to the interior of the state, [some of them as far as Maryland and North Carolina,] where they intermarried with well known families, and their names are found in the records of other parishes. Among the vestrymen of the ancient church at Smithfield, occur the names of Arthur and Thomas Smith; Rev. Charles Smith was Rector of the neighboring parish of Norfolk for upwards of thirty years; and Charles Smith, (who married Margaret Perrin,) removed to Norfolk, where his property was destroyed by the great conflagration during the Revolution. The Perrins probably emigrated from France with the colony of Huguenots,—the widow of one of this family marrying Samuel, eldest brother of Gen. George Washington.

---

[*] The acknowledged head of the Evangelical branch of the Protestant Episcopal Church in the United States.

The following is extracted from the Records of Princess Anne County:
1706, PRINCESS ANNE, ss:

Present, Justice Col. EDWARD MOSELY, Lieutenant-Justice Adam Thorowgood, Major Henry Spratt, Captain Horatio Woodhouse, Mr. John Cornick, Captain Henry Chapman, Captain WILLIAM SMITH, Mr. John Richardson, Captain GEORGE HANCOCK.

It is the record of the trial of Grace Sherwood for witchcraft.

Bishop Meade gives the following account of the former status, and present condition of this venerable Parish:

" Formerly this was one of the most flourishing parishes in Virginia. Many circumstances have concurred to promote its declension. In my early youth I remember to have heard my parents speak of it as having what is called the best society in Virginia. The families were interesting, hospitable, given to visiting and social pleasures. They whose words I quote had some experience of it. Both of them were by marriage connected with the Rev. Anthony Walke, whose mother was a Randolph. At his glebe they were sometimes inmates. The social glass, the rich feast, the card table, the dance, and the horse race, were all freely indulged in through the county. And what has been the result? I passed through the length and breadth of this parish more than twenty years ago, in company with my friend, David Meade Walke, son of the old minister of the parish, who was well acquainted with its past history and present condition, and able to inform me whose were once the estates through which we passed, and into whose hands they had gone; who could point me to the ruins of family seats which had been consumed by fire; could tell me what were the causes of the bankruptcy and ruin, and untimely death of those who once formed the gay society of this county."
The Bishop might have added that this sorrowful state of affairs was the natural outgrowth of slavery, and seems to have been inseperably connected with the institution wherever it was tolerated.

www.ingramcontent.com/pod-product-compliance
Lightning Source LLC
Chambersburg PA
CBHW031117020726
47495CB00007B/2235